The author, Robert Ferguson, is a musician, songwriter, vegetarian, world traveller, writer and animal lover; especially cats. His current aim is to write more novels, which will always have a Scottish theme or connection; concealed somewhere in his writing. He just loves making up curious stories and writing them down. Robert lives in Alloa, Scotland, with his wife, Lorna, dog, Ziggy, cats, Jesse and Roxy. He has a son, Jamie, daughter-in-law, Gemma, granddaughter, Maya, and grandson, Cooper. The Beatles are his FAB 4!

Lorna Ferguson
Travis and their song: Why does it always rain on me.
Glasgow Cabbie, Stef Shaw
Glasgow Museum of Transport
The Panoptican National Theatre, Glasgow
Stan's studio cafe, Sarah J Stanley, Glasgow
Glasgow Humane Society.
Glasgow Police Museum
Glasgow Cathedral
Necropolis, Glasgow
Capercaillie and Servant to the slaves
Formula Rossa, Abu Dhabi
George Harrison and John Lennon
The Glasgow police
The City of Glasgow
The black crow

Robert Ferguson

I'VE GOT JESUS IN THE BACK OF MY TAXI!

A Glasgow Christmas tale

AUSTIN MACAULEY PUBLISHERS™

LONDON • CAMBRIDGE • NEW YORK • SHARJAH

Austin Macauley is committed to publishing works of quality and integrity. In this spirit, we are proud to offer this book to our readers; however, the story, the experiences, and the words are the author's alone.

A CIP catalogue record for this title is available from the British Library.

ISBN 9781528989107 (Paperback)
ISBN 9781528989114 (ePub e-book)

www.austinmacauley.com

First Published (2020)
Austin Macauley Publishers Ltd
25 Canada Square
Canary Wharf
London
E14 5LQ

It's been a long road but we got there. To Lorna, for reading early drafts and giving guidance and encouragement. Jamie, Gemma, Maya and Cooper.

Thanks, Mum and Dad, for a happy childhood. Kisses to Nana, for all those wonderful bedtime stories—they always stayed with me.

The Stranger

It was early December, and heavy snow fell. Glasgow was brimming with festive cheer. Seasonal lights flashed towards trendy George square. Other decorations gently swayed on the tensioned wire which held them in place, and sequenced in a zig-zag course and crossed streets from building to building, which moved in time with a neon sign that protruded from a nearby Georgian type, three-story construction. 'Logan & Lochhead', the animated lights pulsated, flashed and promoted the company name.

The party season was well underway, and this Thursday night was no different, at least, to any other regular Thursday, but festive time always added extra spice and glitter to the occasion. Crowds of partygoers filled pubs, clubs and restaurants, dressed as elves, angels, snowmen and Santa Claus, as they moved joyfully around the city centre, as if in a Xmas convention in some American city. Christmas spirit they call it.

Donald was wrapped warmly, a heavy woollen fair isle sweater was worn under a long black coat, which did more than satisfy his attempt to keep warm, even in the substantial heat of his cab.

His taxi sat at the front of a very long row of taxicabs, waiting for a few more customers to arrive before calling it a night. Parked on West George Street, just a few yards from George Square, a historical area of confluence; a collection of monuments dedicated to Robert Burns, James Watt, Sir Robert Peel and Sir Walter Scott are installed around the old square. Business people took advantage of a few late drinks before heading home. Many stood at the pedestrian crossing opposite Queen Street on the junction of George square, to catch a train to their destination. Stirling? Larbert? Polmont? Alloa? Whatever the end of their journey, most travellers seemed to be full of more than Xmas spirit.

Donald Forbes worked his taxi hard in recent weeks. His energetic effort would be rewarded with a well-earned holiday in early February to somewhere warm to relax, somewhere tranquil where life operated at a slow pace, somewhere less damp, somewhere peaceful, somewhere less hectic, somewhere with not so many shops. His mind took him to a fabulous exotic beach, as he looked intently at drenched, lively partygoers moving around city streets in a joyful, carefree manner; when suddenly, a hand slapped hard against the driver's window.

Donald jumped from his seat with a scared expression fixed on his face, and a surge of adrenaline flowed through his veins which made his heart pound! Turning to see a very drunk young woman staring through the window. Her hair was unkempt and wet, her makeup spoilt by persistent rainfall, giving her a clown-like appearance. In a loud, raspy, voice, she shouted, "Dae ye want a chip?" as her hand once again, slapped against his window, with a grip full of greasy chips, primarily covered in tomato sauce. Her three friends laughed loudly as they staggered forwards, singing a catchy chorus of some 1970s Christmas pop hit. Remnants of a few chips and tomato sauce slowly slid down the window, following raindrops as they slithered downward. Donald mumbled and moaned but knew his taxi had seen many worse sights than a few chips and a tomato condiment plastered over his cab window. Just then, as he was about to exit his cab, (in an attempt) to clean the greasy mess, the rear side door in his Hackney opened, and a soft-spoken voice said,

"Can you take me to Woodlands?"

"Woodlands? Do you have an address?" said Donald inquiringly. He turned his stare to the stranger, who had settled, and continued to stare out the window.

"It has been a few years since I've been in Glasgow. It's such a vibrant fun city." The stranger looked familiar to Donald. Did he know this man?

The street outside flowed with students from a nearby university. All of whom had just started their holiday season and enjoyed a night out before going to homes all over Scotland, and some further afield. Xmas, at parents with all the festive trappings, money from grandparents, was just what they needed.

Glasgow was their natural community during the university semester, and this area was just a short walk to the halls of residence. Pubs were close enough to enable a short stagger home. Cheap beer and food were always an attraction for undergraduates, and the local fish and chip shop would be busy until closing time. A young man, wrapped in a brownish, large duffle coat, attempted to take selfie photographs with every female that had courage enough to pass him. A female police officer was content on getting involved, showing a broad, toothy grin and a thumbs up pose that had the crowd cheering, and a few wolf whistles cut through cold, bitter air to add approval to the situation. Photographs posted on Facebook, Instagram or Twitter would make headlines for a day or so. #glasgowfunpolice.

"Where do you want to go to, sir?" Donald inquired.

Donald stared with great focus at the stranger. The visitor was wearing double denim, had long straight, shoulder length brownish hair which was centre-parted. His beard was long but well-groomed. His eyes were blue, bright as sapphires, even under dull low-level led lights that illuminate the back of the cab, his eyes still shone brightly. "Have we met before?" Donald inquired.

The stranger kept his stare focussed towards people on the street. And without turning, he replied with a charming Glasgow accent, "Many times. Don't you know who I am?"

"No, I don't think I do. But you do look like…" Donald hesitated but stopped talking.

The stranger smiled, turned to face Donald and looked attentively at him, through mainly scratched, damaged Perspex divider, which separated the driver from caged passengers. "You were about to say George Harrison." The stranger returned his gaze street ward which made him grin.

"Yeah, of course, I was about to say George Harrison, how did you know that?" Donald continued, though he couldn't understand why he would hold an immature conversation with his passenger, he did.

"An actual double, if you don't mind me saying. You should start a tribute act, make yourself a fortune. The denim, the hair, the beard and the desert boots. It looks great!" He strangely found himself clasping his hands together and made a praying symbol. With a slight mocking nature, he heard himself say, "Hare Krishna," and laughed slightly but got no response or reaction from his passenger. Not sure why he even did this. His facial expression exposed a feeling of stupidity and guilt.

What am I doing? He cringed ever so slightly.

The outsider interrupted Donald's George Harrison fanciful summary.

"A change of mind, Donald. Take me to Willowbank Primary School."

A push button ignited the engine, a gentle flow of cold air filled his cab, the squeaky, wet, window wipers set in motion a pattern of a slow yet constant cleaning movement that wiped away a continual flow of freezing drizzle. Donald thought for a moment, then turned to face the stranger.

"I was a pupil at Willowbank Primary." He paused slightly, then asked a serious question, "And how on earth do you know my name?"

In an instant, what seemed like a millisecond or maybe less, faster than time itself, his taxi materialised, and sat stationary and correctly parked outside old Willowbank Primary School, just off Woodlands' Road, with Donald sitting, shaking in fear and very unsure of what he had experienced. *What had just happened?* he asked himself. Worn window wipers still grudgingly moved slowly backwards and forwards, and squeaked, as rubber blades hit dry salt spots on the windscreen.

"How did we get here?" he was full of questions. He was lost and felt uncomfortable. *Is this a dream? None of this can be real. It's just beyond belief.*

His mind was in turmoil. How could he comprehend any of this instability to his usual normal day-to-day, mostly mundane life! *Why me?* he thought. How on earth, after sitting in West George Street a few seconds ago, he suddenly appeared here in Woodlands Road? *As if by magic! So, so strange.*

The driver's door clicked open, the stranger stood close by making a motion with his hand for Donald to follow; he spoke sensitively, "I want to show you something, Donald, come with me." The stranger walked off into the night as Donald stepped from his taxi, still shocked and bemused, wondering how he had travelled three miles in seconds, and again, couldn't contemplate what had materialised.

It was if he had sat in a car on the world-famous Formula Rossa, the world's fastest roller coaster based in Abu Dhabi, which reaches speeds of 150 mph and riders experience massive G-force during acceleration and up to 4.8 g throughout the ride. But this was faster! None of this is real! He didn't feel any G-force.

He stood close to the taxi; both hands slapped the roof solidly several times as if seeking confirmation, he was alive, that he wasn't active in a continual looping dream, or a bit player in a science-fiction B movie. He looked warily around the area, still in a lifeless state, shaking his head in a way he did not, or could not, fully understand any reality of what had occurred seconds before. Very quickly, his attention was drawn to the stranger, when the magician's voice sliced through the night air, "Come, Donald."

Donald slammed the door seriously, in a way that would wake up neighbours, and in perfect timing, a dog started barking loudly, which in turn allowed other wakened mutts to join the barking session. His eyes were wide open as his head turned to face the visitor, a fixed or vacant expression smouldered on his cold face. He walked towards him.

"What has just happened, am I dead?" he spoke in a weary-sounding, desperate shaking voice.

"No, you are fine. I want to show you this space. Do you know this building?" The stranger waited for a reply.

Donald stared at the old school façade. Blinking his eyes briefly before deciding if he should verbally offer words, though unimaginable thoughts that were flowing en masse through his head. He did speak, however, "The school was old and been derelict for years. A local private developer renovated the dilapidated building into these very lavish apartments, I believe." He paused.

"I have many great memories of this place."

Donald stared keenly at the old red brick frontage.

"Is this some weird Christmas Carol type of game we are playing? I get to see my life in its past, present or a possible future?"

"Is this what this is all about, or am I going mad and all of this is a disturbing dream, are you an angel or something different?"

The stranger held out his long-fingered hand and, in an intended motion, raised it towards Donald, spoke affectionately, "Take my hand, Donald," and in an instant, both were standing in a classroom, of a time Donald recognised, a class he knew, his memory suddenly recalled his past, thoughts flooded his open mind with events he had all but lost or forgotten.

He stood and stared at his class of 1970, frozen in time, like marble statues in an Italian museum, possibly the Uffizi in Florence sprung to mind. It was like viewing a three-dimensional image of his past. All his classmates appearing before him, and he was part of this classroom once again. *It was forever strange,* he thought.

Uniforms, the children sported, were predominately grey, though a splatter of colours shone from girls' blouses and a few boys' ties. Of course, this was December 1970, and younger teachers and children alike showed a rebellious side that was a gift to all that generation. 1970s fashion produced large, lurid coloured prints, which were mainly used for wallpaper design and hoped to turn any mundane living room into a discotheque. These designs were meant to exude fun and a sense of liberty, characterising off-beat design style of the decade.

A great teenage rebellion of course. It's Glam rock and all that! Get it on, bang a gong, and get it on! In the early 70s, particularly in public schools, young, energetic teachers rebelled against school dress rules, growing their hair long, wearing jeans and being down with the kids. Miss Turner was no different. Her red, Christian Dior Roll Neck Jumper kept her warm and flared C&A jeans added to 70s fashion. The 1970s platform boots had heels in many assorted sizes, and Miss Turner's stature rose by three inches. Any other type of boot could have platforms, but these boots gave added winter protection to style, which was a requirement for her. Her straight hair was the current way to wear long hair, as seen on actress, Ali McGraw, a year later in 1971, award-winning movie, *Love Story* was released, which was nominated for seven Academy Awards, winning one: Best Music, Original Score – Francis Lai, a French songwriter and composer.

Most pupils were wearing warm, thick woolly jumpers or similar jerseys, or V-neck tank tops, in a complicated layering endeavour that worked for some children but not for others, layers that covered nylon shirts and cotton vests. Boys wore long trousers for further cold protection. Girls, on the other hand, had a variety of winter clothes and accessories, with warm leggings and wellies amongst many items. School heaters that had been functioning well before lessons started and had managed to build up sizeable storage of heat. The antiquated heater system that surrounded the room lay in two horizontal rows of cast iron piping and showed many years of hardened layers of paint which smothered the plumbing. All of this made the pipes look more significant than their actual size. A multitude of clothing suppresses nearly all available space of the heater system. Anoraks, duffle coats, Tammie's, scarfs and gloves, all sitting, slumped in bundles, drip-drying. Occasionally, a high-pitched squeaking noise emanated from the burdened water-filled cylinders as if an old man would complain about his back pain. Donald could smell mixed odours, as wet clothing dried releasing smells that usually indicated that moisture had settled for an extended period in a warming room. Strong, pungent smells added to this strange experience.

Empty milk bottles sat in a crate near the classroom door. Donald noticed that a few bottles remained untouched. He remembered that in days of cold winter, when school milk froze, it gave a protruding flow of expanding milked ice that raised the silver foil cap off at an angle, which made it look, in some strange way, like a drunken soldier attempting to stand to attention. Children's drawings and paintings scattered the walls. A large, plastic, or possibly waxed world map was suspended with tin tacks and had distributed notes attached. A chalk-covered duster sat prominently on a small shelf, or wooden mount, that lay in the front of the chalkboard. Some teachers used this eraser as a missile or deterrent for the more pestilent, or annoying children and launch the duster towards the nuisance child.

The class looked real, he thought. But it's like a pause button had been pressed halfway through a film, or a TV show. All frozen in one moment in time. A time that Donald recognised!

"This is my old class; I was about eight or nine. That's Miss Turner!" he said pointing to the young teacher. "And there's John Gray, and there's Davie Stewart." His eyes widened, as his gaze was searching the room and recalling names of his classmates.

"Listen to this, Donald," the stranger said as the class erupted instantly and came to life. Immediately, the scene burst forth into action. He was back in 1970.

Miss Turner spoke as she sat on the edge of her desk. "Who would you like to be like when you are older, and why would you like to be like this person?" Miss Turner had also written this statement on the blackboard.

She pointed her small square forefinger, which a palmist once told her, in addition to being square, she had a good sense of order, and a realistic approach to life and a love of all things punctual. All of which was true.

"Ruth!" she pointed to an identified her first choice.

Ruth was a small stout girl, self-contained, in a tight-fitting, frock dress. A yellow checked ribbon, unsuccessfully, held her dry, frizzy, long, brown hair in place, in a home-made bun, that sat awkwardly on top of her head. Her mouth and lips showed stained remnants of some sugary food coloured dyed sweet. A sweet she may have devoured before class started, or possibly during lessons, from a well-hidden stash of goodies that lay inside a desk full of assorted sweets. Treats that many a tuck shop would be proud to hold.

Her small frame stood tall. As high as her toes could get her, though she floundered as she attempted to straighten her tight-fitting dress, which she hoped would show her classmates a perfect view of her performance. And with an air of know-it-all confidence, she fluttered bird-like, to get her well-rehearsed point over. And she did. With a cute and courteous Glasgow accent, she released her unfeigned vocal cords.

She began to read from her small blue Silvine exercise jotter, which was covered in household wallpaper. *It showed a pattern of yellow and orange floral circular designs that would light up any dark room,* Miss Turner thought. She read as a professional actor would, if rehearsing for a significant acting role. Without many stopping points or breathing spaces, Ruth belted out her well-rehearsed story.

"Miss, I would like to be like Lulu as she is a beautiful singer. She was born in Lennoxtown, in East Dunbartonshire, and grew up in Dennistoun like us. She also sang *Boom Bang a Bang* in the Eurovision song competition and came joint-first winner with two other entries."

Ruth scarcely took another breath. Catching a quick lungful made the children giggle. Some pronunciation was dubious, but Miss Turner did not intervene or point out any mistake. Ruth and her story were unrelenting.

So, she continued with her story,

"Lenny Kuhr singing *De Troubadour* for the Netherlands, Salome was singing *Vivo Cantando* for Spain, and Frida Boccara singing *Un jour, un enfant* for France. This song also charted at number two in the UK charts and did well all over

Europe." Ruth inhaled enough air to fill several balloons as she accepted applause with a toothy smile. Her face was red as a summer apple.

"Well done, Ruth," spoke Miss Turner. "A round of applause, please." She enthusiastically encouraged the class to join her in appreciation. Children clapped and stamped their cold feet on beech flooring as if watching a talent show.

The adult Donald was surprised to hear a girl so young, a girl he remembered as ordinarily lazy, who would avoid Gym or playground activities at the best of times, could even pronounce words Ruth had just promoted to her class. He was impressed and clapped his hands in appreciation but felt foolish doing so.

Ruth, as he recalled, was always a bright spark, but only ever interested in studies she liked. Donald nodded in recognition of remembering her stand-out performance. On leaving school, she would work at a local John Menzies store on Argyll Street, and years later, manage the music department, of course! Living her dream of being the most knowledgeable sales assistant in any music department in history; his memory reimbursed his current thoughts.

"I'm sure I bought a few albums from her at some point," he recalled, "I'm also sure she won a significant quiz on TV in the 80s. I believe it was *Mastermind*? Her specific subject was Eurovision, of course."

The children responded with furious hand clapping and laughter as Ruth bundled her frame forcibly on to the seat, showing and promoting a face full of pride and achievement. Now, the class were taking an active role, they knew how impulsive this game could be, how each child could become anyone they wanted to be, a sporting hero, a movie star, a pop star, a comic book hero. There was no need to prompt the children now; they were leaping from their chairs and trying to jump as high as possible, as they attempted to gain eye contact with Miss Turner. Repeating, "Miss, Miss, Miss," which was also a valuable tool for any school child that wanted to be seen or heard.

Among the chaos of screaming excited children, Miss Turner pointed to Eddie Hall.

Eddie Hall, the class joker and playground comedian, the boy with a thousand voices, master of trips and tumbles, and future club-land entertainer, was chosen. The children sat silently awaiting Eddie's story.

"Miss, I want to be just like Stan Butler from on the buses, so I could drive big buses around Glasgow and have lots of fun."

Though usually a self-confident boy, this restricted scenario became a bit too much for him and, suddenly, lost nerve. There were no more words to offer, his mind drew a blank and he shook ever so slightly as he looked around the class to see classmates staring keenly at him.

Although a few fumbled words more were spoken, he could no longer access the type of thoughts his story required. His relaxed concerns got the better of him and he froze.

Eddie sat down before losing further control of the situation or being jeered by his previously developed audience; he anxiously imagined.

For one time only, Eddie Hall was lost for words. A time that he would never repeat!

The class, in their happy mood, tapped their desks and giggled as Eddie started to broadcast his nerves in the usual form, by unwittingly have his face turned a red, brownish colour, which lit the room. His nickname was then and would remain, into adulthood, the Chestnut.

Unexpectedly, a small, rectangular, well-used eraser thrown at speed, and with perfect aim, bounced off his sleepy head which made him scream aloud, and with immediate reaction and reasoned response, used both his hands to rub his head frantically, in a hope to ease the pain.

Miss Turner warned the class of these unrequited actions, but they remained joyous and unsettled.

Alex Wood promoted himself to be next in line, by spurting out his thoughts before teacher's square finger hovered or pointed in his direction.

"Miss, I would like to be like Butch Cassidy. Making loads of money by robbing banks and riding fast horses. Living in the wild west, having lots of guns and getting involved in gunfights."

All children sniggered again.

"I'm sure he was jailed later in life for armed robbery. His role model seemingly stuck with him," said Donald in a sarcastic way. "How ironic," he added.

The adult Donald turned to face Miss Turner as he heard his name mentioned.

"Donald, what about you?" she said. The class turned to look towards the child Donald.

He was quiet and unresponsive. He was in thought.

"Can you tell the class who you would like to be and why?" said Miss Turner as she strolled towards Donald's desk which sat to the rear of the class. His classmates were quiet and focused their eyes on him.

The stranger and Donald stood and watched more situation unravel as viewers of a small stage play. Close to the action. Part of the scenario.

Young Donald slowly pushed his chair back and stood. His trousers showed several splits and ragged tears around the knees; an ageing aunt had knitted his jumper, which would probably fit a boy several years older. His hair was short, back and sides cut, with a long, scruffy fringe hovering around his eyes. What is a comb? And, as usual, a colourful tie wrapped around his neck was not a school tie but a football supporter's relationship! It promoted his favourite football team! The class and Miss Turner waited with bated breath, to hear Donald's response.

"I, I want to be like Jesus," he said with a little soft voice that not many of the class heard, nor Miss Turner. A few classmates that did detect his choice of words spread the news to others, and a chain reaction of muffled giggles erupted.

"Can you tell us again, Donald? We didn't hear what you said," Miss Turner intervened the chatter and laughing, and warned them to remain silent.

"I want to be like Jesus, miss," he said in a much louder voice. "I-want-to-be-like-Jesus," he repeated slowly but louder. The class was now silent, and all stared in Donald's direction. They began to sit. He spoke again, "I want to be like Jesus so that I can help people. I can help people that don't have money, give them food and heat their cold house. I would also bring my dad back to life." Donald returned to his seat and pulled his small chair back under him. He sat silent. The class sat silent. The children did not know how to respond to Donald's story.

Just then, a bell rang loud to intrude the moment, a very surreal moment that Donald returned to face again, but this time as an adult. The class erupted, all the children suddenly forgot Donald's communication and the importance of it, even if it meant nothing much to any of them – whether it had significance to Donald either.

A little melee darted en route on the pathway to freedom, with Miss Turner advising them to make way from class carefully. None of them listened, as children fought through a small door space.

Donald remained static, sitting in his little wooden seat, with his face looking down on his desktop.

The stranger turned to Donald. "Do you remember this moment?"

The scene was on pause again.

Donald was staring at his younger self. "Yes, I do. My dad had died a few months earlier. My mum never got over his death, none of us did. It was the worst Christmas we ever had. Our lives changed forever. We didn't have Dad's wages anymore, Mum got a little job working part-time in a bakery initially and worked tirelessly for many years in many low-paid, part-time jobs. Some in bars, shoe shops, a local cinema some nights, Timothy Whites on one occasion, and a few years at Copeland & Lyle."

By reminiscing further, it brought more information back to mind.

"I used to nip into Copland & Lyle after secondary school to watch a sales assistant pack the bill and insert the money in some strange glass tube contraption that fired a container through pipes with a loud 'whoosh', and a receipt came back through this infernal machine about half an hour later. It was space age. Kinda like *Star Trek*. But I loved it!" he continued.

"We struggled in those early days after Dad died. Then in 1971, Mum moved us to a small flat in Dennistoun, to be nearer her sister, she said. My brother and I attending Alexander Parade primary school, and had to make a whole lot of new friends. Which we did.

"We were always fed and clothed and taken care of, but life was never the same again. Not hearing his bad jokes anymore, or his creative bedtime stories, playing football in the local park; just having Dad around, but then he was gone! Our holidays at Butlin's were special when he was alive. We went to Ayr holiday camp every Glasgow Fair. I'll never forget those happy times. Memories are flooding back to me just standing here."

The stranger was looking at a child's drawing attached to the wall. It depicted two boys swinging on a rope swing attached to an enormous oak tree, perched on a small green hill.

He spoke, "You and your brother, John, it looks fun."

"I can't remember painting that."

"It has your name printed on the bottom," he continued, "looks like lots of fun."

Donald paused as if he didn't want to mention the drawing or its meaning, but he did.

"It was a week or so after Dad died, we were at Nana Forbes house in Kilsyth. Just a weekend to get us away from Glasgow, they said. It was the first time we had laughed, and we both felt guilty."

"Really, for having fun?"

"Our mum was still in a terrible way. She wasn't coping too well with Dad's death, and we were out enjoying ourselves," he explained.

"I believe the sentiment and thought of young Donald were splendid." The stranger touched Donald's right shoulder and spoke,

"One, Timothy – Let no man despise thy youth; but be thou an example of the believers, in a word, in conversation, in charity, in spirit, in faith, in purity."

Donald looked into the bright blue eyes of the stranger. "Who are you? Is this punishment for a young schoolboy speaking his mind? Are you an angel?"

The stranger stared directly into Donald's eyes and his initial reaction was to feel a warm glow flow through him.

"I am Jesus. The man you wanted to be," he said, as he took Donald's hand, both dissolved from the classroom and returned in an instant to the taxi; a surreal movement which once again astonished Donald.

"What about some food?" said Jesus. "Some tasty takeaway," as he sat comfortably in the rear of the taxi.

Again, Donald was dumbfounded by the way he was shuffling around space and time, here one minute and gone the next. None of this sideshow made sense. *I am sure all of this is a dream caused by an extreme fever of some sort, and I will awaken at any time*, he still believed these thoughts.

He heard the stranger mention food, to which he replied,

"Food?" Donald answered inquisitively, as he looked directly at him. He looked bemused. Still lost in the moment.

Rubbing his eyes, he hoped he would wake up from this strange, very dreamlike delusion.

"You say you are Jesus. Do you mean the real Jesus?"

"Yes, of course, I am. Let's get some nice food. You choose, whatever food you prefer," said Jesus, as he sat back to enjoy whatever view came to him.

Donald pressed the ignition button again and anticipated another sudden dissolving act, as he pressed both eyes tightly in expectation of the move, but it didn't happen. He drove towards the city centre. This time, however, he did manage to cover the full distance by road, and not disappear and re-appear instantaneously. But still perplexed by this situation. He drove in silence, though Jesus chatted about sites and buildings of Glasgow, all of which he didn't hear; his mind was elsewhere.

Donald couldn't evaluate any of this; he felt outlandish in this mixture of truths and some virtual reality which were held within realms of science fiction or possibly beyond all of this. But it was true, an imaginary school class scenario was as factual as he could recall, and furthermore, it was even more than he could remember. It was all exact and to the point. He continued to drive, still silent in thought.

The city was now in the early part of Friday morning. Glasgow, like most cities at this time of day, seemed deserted and slept. However, a few stragglers are always part of the makeup of Glasgow at this early hour, and some well-oiled walkers, wandered aimlessly, looking for food or a dark coffee; to prove another point that apart from New York, Glasgow also doesn't sleep!

An ambulance with pulsating blue lights drove at speed towards Glasgow Royal as it flew past Donald's taxi, spitting up rain from the puddles it rolled through. There have been a few council rubbish trucks starting to clean the streets for yet another working day which lay ahead. Emptying garbage by tilting large business wheelie bins into the back of a smelly, heavy laden truck. Weary workers buzzed everywhere escorting big garbage containers to the stationary vehicle and other workers returning empty silos to the safety of the pavement. The wagon had some chain or wire, to strap and hold containers in place, which then lifted two hollows on the back portion of the vehicle. Through space, waste then slid in the tray to show a multitude of garbage, then a few disturbingly, noisy shakes created by the mechanism, forced leftovers of rubbish into the brimming waste deposit. One sanitation worker wore a Santa hat that had a flashing bauble; the cap looked too big for him. He whistled as he worked.

A few angry seagulls followed the operation in a military-style fashion, in a slight hope to collect any dropped pizza box or takeaway carton, which would hopefully contain some crust or possibly a slice of Hawaiian or Margherita, or perhaps chips with red sauce. One seagull got lucky. A mass of his feathery comrades hunted him down for what looked like a precious gift of a small green olive. The small fruit was smartly devoured as he sat quietly on a street corner, which made the pursuing army give high pitch cawing voices of disapproval. He shook his head as the discovered treat was swallowed whole. A further shake gave a sign of a disgusting, repulsive taste, or maybe enjoyment! Other seagulls looked despondent but returned aggrieved to the field of operations with a hope of starting the game once again. The game restarted! A bedraggled single crow was a sole spectator in all this action as the adaptable gulls squabbled over other discovered titbits. Maybe the crow was looking and learning.

Instantly, Donald's daydream broke as he launched both his size ten working boots forwards, they slowly stuck and latched onto the brake and clutch instantaneously, which then initiated a highly quick emergency stop. A moment in time, when his head kissed the windscreen, and his chest and arms revolved uncontrollably around the cabin void as if swimming. The pulling force of inertia reel seatbelt hauled him back into the mixed fabric and leather seat. Even in these conditions, the stop was fast. Very fast! He let out a high pitch girly scream which I'm sure he didn't notice.

He sat for a moment.

He had just bore witness to killing Jesus. He must have hit him. The vehicle was doing 30 mph!

"Jesus was standing in front of my taxi. I must have hit him! I've run over Jesus," he mumbled.

He tensely turned to look in the back, but Jesus was gone.

Departing his taxi slowly, and by the scared, grimaced look on his face, he didn't want to see a product of his slow reactions, Jesus under his taxi. Or worse, a dead Jesus laying on the road. He started a fearful search around the cab, even putting his hands on the icy, wet road, as he struggled down to look beneath the vehicle. After a walk around the car, he saw no one, far less Jesus.

"Where is Jesus?" he said tearfully.

At this moment, unnoticed, or even seen, appearing from a bright yellow and blue Battenberg vinyl patterned police van, which sat only a few feet behind his taxi, stood two police officers. Both burly male Glasgow cops, a sergeant, in his mid-fifties, and the other, no more than a rookie, both looked slightly overweight and more than a few rope skips from a healthy and fit lifestyle, or possibly too many after-shift beers added unrequired extra pounds. Large hi-vis jackets gave the appearance of outsized frames within, both no-nonsense Glasgow cops all the same. But, as usual in their trade, combined with Glasgow service and dealing with daily banter from locals, had a gift, or more importantly, a Glasgow gift of having a comedic repartee. They approached Donald. Donald stared at both officers as an unassured expression froze over his emotionless, blank and guilty looking face.

"If you are drunk or not. Was Mickey Mouse a cat or a dog?" said the officer wearing sergeant stripes on either arm and fully not expecting any reply to his question, it was a sarcastic statement, not a request. The other officer stood formally next to his colleague as if both were a music hall double act. Donald offered a reasonable explanation. He thought he did!

"I have not been drinking, officer, I thought I hit something or somebody," presented Donald in a weak nervous voice.

"If it weren't for my quick reaction, we would be pulling our halogen headlights out of your arse," the sergeant threw his booming voice towards Donald. And by a sickened response, Donald's head gave way, reversing back slightly, sniffing every breath from the policeman's mouth, as it hit his face in warm waves of fried onions or garlic.

"I thought I ran over someone. I saw someone standing a few feet in front of my taxi," Donald's weak smile gaped from his face as he pointed to the front of his taxi.

The younger officer used his small black torch, to illuminate light around the vehicle. A short walk, to double check for an injury, or possibly a fatality; showed nobody. "My takeaway is getting cold," he muttered under his breath.

"Can you tell me what this person looked like?" the sergeant forced his powerful voice once again with still warm, garlic blasting towards Donald's scowling face.

Donald thought for a moment. He spoke as if he didn't want to answer. But he thought, *The truth is best. Just be honest!*

"Well, in a strange way, he looked like George Harrison: from The Beatles. You know, the quiet one?" He waited for a response or possibly a small plastic tube forcibly inserted or violently plunged into his now dry mouth. He closed his mouth shut in preparation as the thought crossed his mind, but never expected the response he received.

"Like the person sitting in your taxi, sir?" said the young officer as his torch shone the beam into the rear of the cab, with the last energy radiating from a dwindling light source of cheap batteries

The officer swung the door open, confirming, a lookalike sitting comfortably and far from being a victim of a hit and run.

Donald turned, then sloped his head slightly to one side, this gave him a clear view past the broad frame of the fat sergeant, which provided a clear picture of his passenger who looked very much alive and unhurt.

And by this, he was able to see Jesus sitting relaxed, smiling and granting a slow waving hand motion towards himself and both officers. The lower jaw on Donald's chilled face plummeted as far as it could drop. His eyes fixed on Jesus.

The police officers saw Jesus in the back of my taxi! Just as I do. His rotating thoughts jammed his mental processes. *So, Jesus is real! This man can be seen by the officers, and I'm not going mad!*

The young Bobby, with an expected, yet a non-required voice of attempted authority, spoke to Jesus, "Evening, sir. Did you witness a person or persons standing in front of the taxi before it suddenly came to a forced stop?" (Which more than likely threw the officers freshly bought takeaway food over the dashboard and floor, as they too stopped extraordinarily fast.)

"I'm so sorry, officer, I didn't look ahead. I was too busy viewing the illuminated buildings and the beautiful Christmas lights," said Jesus in a broad, thick Glaswegian accent.

"And where are you heading, sir – if I may inquire?" he probingly added, doing his utmost to close this situation off, then return to the warmth of his van and hopefully end this hard shift; they had supper to eat!

"I'm here to meet Donald," he said nodding his head towards the bemused figure that stood close by.

The sergeant knew he was the person to deal with this situation, so he aggressively walked towards the taxi and stuck his massive head inside to gain sanctuary from the persistent drizzle and to have a more unobstructed view of the passenger. He didn't use his torch. The batteries were low. He asked the stranger three questions without taking a breath of air.

"So, you are here to meet with the taxi driver? Have you been a passenger in his cab all night? Or did you jump in recently?" he said in an abrupt and unswervingly harsh manner. He wants to finish his shift and not spend any more time with a pair of numpties he thought.

"Aye, yes, I'm here to play catch up with Donald. I've been in his taxi for possibly an hour or so, just to cruise the sites of Glasgow. I'm happy looking at the beautiful architecture and historical sites. It's been years since I've been in Glasgow. I really should visit more. The festive lights look lovely; don't you think?"

The officer gave a glance out the back window looking at some old buildings. His facial grimaces showed that architecture was not one of his prime priorities. With a grunt of disapproval, he inhaled a long breath of air and exhaled through pouted lips; as a dull, boring response.

Jesus spoke,

"Well, if I am honest to you, and to put all my cards on the table. I did expect to see you tonight also.

"I believe you are thinking about early retirement and possibly a move to the coast? Somewhere near a beach, a harbour, a few excellent restaurants and, of course, the obligatory pub."

Jesus said teasingly,

"You are in two minds and cannot decide between either Anstruther or St Andrews. Two of my favourites also. Both have similar attributes, I must say. Golf courses at St Andrews is a great attraction, but Anstruther is a must for a fish supper. Don't you agree?"

The sergeant shook his head slowly, and a smile appeared over his broad, Cro-Magnon, face.

"Well done! I get it now. The guys at the station put you jokers on my case. A big wind up! Excellent, splendid indeed. Aye, but you forgot to say that golf is not my main hobby and I haven't hit a ball in years, plus the fact is, I've got Broughty Ferry in my mind as a further choice.

"You didn't hear that, did you?"

He moved back from the cab towards the street.

"I must admit it was all a bit strange at first, but now I get it. Just wait till I get back to the station and let them know that there is no way anyone can pull the wool over Ian Shaw's eyes. Hey, good job, guys. Full marks!"

His attention turns to Donald, "You and George Harrison can get on your way and enjoy touring the sights. Remember to tell your pals at Anderston Station you failed in your assignment."

He smiled as he walked to his van, stopped and turned to face Donald and spoke, "Have a good day, guys." Mockingly waving as the taxi began to move.

"I didn't have anything to do with this, sarge, I promise," said the young constable as both returned to the police van. He added, "I never heard any of the guys plotting to wind you up, sarge." The sergeant ignores his comments, as the constable continued to blether more and more in his defence or his involvement in any deception. The sergeant sat smirking with a no one gets the better of me, kind of look.

The young officer's attention was swiftly drawn to space on the seat next to him and sees one large bag of piping hot food.

He taps his boss on the arm and points down to the food bag. Sergeant Shaw ignored his initial intrusion and kept his stare at the taxi disappearing in the distance. "They must think they are funny," he said flippantly. "Smart my arse!" he further added.

The young officer tapped his shoulder again, and this time, Sergeant Shaw turned his disgruntled attention towards him.

"What?" was his full immediate response to having his shift disrupted by two complete strangers, and have an irritating young officer add to his bad day at the office.

The young Bobby remained silent and pointed a poking finger towards the carrier bag.

Shaw's attention was drawn to the object that sat upright on the seat space between them, eyed the container intently for a few seconds until a surprised and frightened look appeared on his face, he looked into the eyes of the young constable, but neither spoke. His gaze fell to the floor and dashboard, searching for fragments or remnants of chicken tikka or mushroom omelette, or onion rings that he knew too well had splattered most of the interior. A clean-up operation, they both were dreading, would not now commence.

The sergeant leisurely picked up the warm brown carrier bag, suspiciously looked inside and saw a food order, just like the takeaway they had purchased and had previously started to eat, and surely witnessed flying around the interior; some minutes before. At least, it smelled identical.

A small paper note was attached to the yellow plastic carton which he ripped off and held up to his face, close enough to read.

"You will love St Andrews."

The sergeant's loud voice filled the night air! "WHAT THE F..."

The Old Charity Shop

It was 9.00 am, it was cold but dry. Donald strained to see through the drying windscreen which required regular screen wash solution sprayed to clear his view. He imagined continual driving around the city, for what seemed like hours. Round and around empty city streets, the same stop and start irritant of maddening traffic lights dotted on every road in the city centre, which drove taxi driver's crazy and regular motorists alike. Hordes of delivery trucks and white vans parked wherever they could achieve a space, all in a similar rush and to get close to their drop-off point. Wheelbarrows and small pallet trucks screeching in and out of delivery doors. Drivers attempting to write on the problematic electronic handheld devices, where they enter delivery details and participant name, quietly waiting to sign it off by scribbling nonsense on a small screen, so they also can get back to the job they are paid to do. Sign and send, then off to the next delivery.

Buses were now working their routes, pedestrians arriving in droves from either the railway, subway, bus or car or just walkers that live close to the city centre. More taxis now were buzzing about streets like busy bumble bees looking for the next flower to feast. Donald's head was still in silent mode. His mind kept filling with many images and thoughts. He occasionally looked in the rear-view mirror that showed Jesus, or where the magician with incredible magical powers sat, waving his hands around as he grinned at the view of more beautiful buildings, structures they passed street after street. Donald heard him Jesus talking and talking. *If this man is Jesus, then I have let him chatter away without responding.* He felt guilty. But flashes of tropical beaches constantly interrupted his thoughts. A long golden beach with palm trees swaying in the breeze, blue ocean propelling white foaming surf over the golden sand, time after time, still white after white, and as always, excess water sucked back into the on-coming sea after a continuous delivery that forever endures, in and out as always. He saw beautiful birds hovering above him. *Possibly laughing gulls,* he thought. But he didn't know too much about birds or species like them. Why did he mention laughing gulls?

He awakened from his micro slumber as the voice of Jesus became loud and clear. He was awake now. Jesus spoke,

"Park in the space to the left, Donald."

Although mystified, Donald was now alert and ready for the next stage of this continuing fantasy.

The taxi manoeuvred into a perfect size space with room to spare at either end. Donald's cumbersome and ungainly steps followed Jesus from the cab, as both walked towards a shop.

Donald paid some attention to many patches of hardened gum stuck to the pavement, as a street sweeper glided a brush over the unmovable mess – but managed to pick up a few loose pieces of litter and other forms of accessible debris that was gathered and dropped into a council wheelie bin.

Donald viewed a charity shop before him. It seemed very Victorian in style. It had vintage cream painted exterior walls with two large glass-framed windows separated by an ornate door. Dressed mannequins and bric-a-brac filled each window. An elaborate, beautiful panelled door had a four-pane grill arch above it that housed a decorative, deep coloured, stained glass insert, which looked stunning in the morning light. A bright well-designed sign that sat on a fascia above the shop front said: *A Heart for the Homeless.* A slogan was identified in either window with white vinyl promoting promotional words: *A small charity with a big heart.*

The design and natural look of the shop completed a marriage of style and poise, which the charitable foundation wanted to achieve in its presentation. A small Glasgow based charity that had struggled in recent times, with either a lack of high-quality donations or deep-pocket sponsors, to maintain a steady flow of income or at least keep up a healthy balance in the charities bank account.

Indeed, most charity users preferred charity shops that hold brand or popular designer items. And not cheaper clothes types or clothes more akin to older mature types of wear which was the bulk of stock their small storeroom held. Some younger shoppers used the tag, 'Grannies rags', whenever they mentioned the site on social media. If a fancy-dress night was on the cards, and vintage clothing the identifying mark, then this was the place to dress for the occasion.

As they walked closer to the shop entrance, Donald stopped, turned his head to see a paid parking ticket already stuck on the windscreen of his cab. *Another unexplained mystery,* he thought. *I wonder if the fuel tank is full*; entered his guilty mind.

The shop had a small team of volunteers, all work part-time and for the love of charity. They had, for many years, sold hundreds of items donated by loyal supporters, including second-hand men and women's clothing, and a variety of one-off relics from a time past. Not to mention, second-hand homewares, vintage dresses, vinyl records, toys, books and a few large cartons of old jigsaws with many missing pieces and more, much more. A few years earlier, someone donated an ugly vase with unusual colourway design. But after an eagle-eyed member of staff, a veteran of viewing antique shows on TV thought it could be worth more than the £3.00 ticket price stuck on its base. They decided to have it valued and authenticated. It was, in fact, excellent quality.

Thankfully, it was soon discovered to be a 1930s Clarice Cliff Lotus jug, and fortunately, it sold for £5,600. A tidy sum for any charity, but for them, it was another lifeline. Keeping the wolves from the doors for a wee while only one staff member said.

Jesus was in the process of opening the door when he stopped suddenly, stood still on the geometric and encaustic Victorian tiled entrance, pointed upwards, and said, "Listen to this magical device, Donald." Then he opened the door.

When the door opened a few inches, it set in motion a three-chime doorbell apparatus, it rang, being triggered by a latch attached to the door frame. The bells were standard ones, not electric, and they made a characteristic, 'ting, ting, ting, all in tandem'. An alarm system that told the shopkeeper a customer had arrived or had left – a bell system that has been ringing since 1894, where Gordon M Feather ran a tobacconist outlet from this site and from this shop. Some shoppers say the old mahogany wall cabinets, that now display small object d'art, has an unyielding scent of Old Dutch brandy dipped cigars.

A quaint little shop, where age-old bell door chimes added an actual substance to an era no longer here. Jesus enjoyed the sound of the bell chimes as he entered the shop with Donald tagging intently behind him.

"Good morning, can I help you?" said the little-spoken voice of Edna Hughes, a 72-year-old spinster, who daily makes a journey from her Partick home to St Enoch's station on the clockwork orange, or Glasgow subway, to give the train system its proper name, on her weekly excursion to work, taking about twelve minutes on a decent day. Though depending on movement, she found weekends much more bountiful of traffic, and her trip took much longer.

"Yes," Jesus said, as he pointed to an abundance of men's suits all hanging, tightly bunched, on a static display stand with chrome fittings, all of which sat on four roller castors. "Can I have that black suit please?" he said in a precise manner, as he stood a few feet from the display.

Edna approached the stand still looking for validation that she was choosing correctly. Many different shades of black and grey, with a few lighter materials dotted throughout the massed group of clothes. It would take a length of time to search through each suit crammed onto the strained, bending rail that supported used and worn stock.

She aimlessly laid her hands on the first jacket her hand chose, looking for confirmation that she may be near the suit the customer requested.

"That's the one," Jesus said as Edna took a closer look at the jacket and gave an expression of surprise, that she had placed her hand on the selected suit from many similar ones.

A pure guess, she thought. She opened the jacket to check the suit size that she knew too well would be printed on a small rectangular tag sewn on the pocket. The brand name, the size, the material used to produce the garment were all stated on this universal clothing informative label.

"Medium, is this the suit, sir?" her perfect, quaint Glasgow accent filtered through the room as she looked at the stranger and sought approval.

"That is just perfect," confirmed Jesus. He placed a pair of black brogues and a plain white shirt, a nondescript purple tie and a new pair of black cotton socks that he had picked up from nearby units sitting near the checkout.

Edna took the items and prepared to put them in a large carrier bag.

"Are these items for you, sir?" she enquired and added,

"The suit is excellent quality."

"No, it's a very dear friend who has been down on his luck recently. I thought a present would cheer him up," Jesus deliberately made his point and added, "He once was a dance instructor and choreographer for many years. He spent many summer seasons at Butlin's in Ayr where he taught to dance." Possibly looking for a reaction from Edna.

Donald was consuming information but didn't understand the ideology or take any belief in the situation he faced, nor did he fully understand any part of it. Not yet anyway. He stood as a spectator. He watched and listened. Not caring about missed customers he may have lost in the past several hours. Or potential customers that may be looking for an urgent pick up as he stood playing a minor role in all this madness.

"That's interesting," said Edna. "My late husband, John, and I spent many wonderful holidays in Ayr. It was lovely there. We went year on year. Many happy days spent there, I can tell you, with many fond memories." She was smiling and thinking of a time long gone. "Goodness me, I have many boxes of photographs and cine film to recall every beautiful moment of our memorable holidays."

Edna was reminiscing. She never managed to have full conversations with younger customers. They were continually conversing on phones most of the time. She let happy thoughts flood out to the two strangers. She was folding the suit and gently placed each item into the carrier bag.

"Butlin's in Ayr! What a great place for a holiday," offered Jesus.

"Oh, yes. The holiday camp was so special back in its heyday. There was a huge swimming pool, a great outdoor pool which was full most of the day. Mind you, it was icy cold most of the time, even in the best of summer days, it was a challenge, just thinking about a swim." She was smiling now and happily reminisced recalled memories. "Though children would jump, dive, splash and frolic at all depths of the pool. Their yelling little voices echoed around the camp. The glory of youth I guess." Edna was in full flow now.

"They kept the miserable lifeguard busy and alert at all times, and he used most of his strength blowing a metal whistle, that hung around his neck, in anticipation of stopping an unruly child. After gaining attention from a guilty child, he would furiously point a waving finger towards the culprit, as the high pitch signal let out a bellowing screeching noise that drew attention from most in the pool and many within fifty yards or so. He would scream aloud the laws, at any culprit not obeying the strict rules and regulations, which he had memorised by heart; a threat of dismissal from the pool was the best option most of the time. A red card after several warnings usually did the trick. I always thought that, after a full day's work, the lifeguard would sleep for hours. In a sleepless struggle, having a full-on nightmare that gave an unpleasant dream where he attempted to keep a strict policy intact though no one would ever take heed of his efforts. Poor man, I thought!

"Mind you, we would have done the same when we were younger, I'm sure," Edna just kept talking.

"John and I loved the old-time ballroom dancing. We had lessons from many an exceptional instructor, and a fantastic band played popular hits and enduring classics rang out as we danced all day. We entered a competition one year, and though we were nowhere near the best dancers, we won! Maybe they appreciated our willingness to keep trying year in, year out."

She realised she had been chattering too much and possibly the customers were not sold on her anecdotes.

She apologised, "I'm sorry, I don't know what came over me. Chatting away like a songbird." She looked embarrassed. "It's not like me to exchange stories like that. I just couldn't stop. I do apologise."

Jesus intervened on Edna's apology. "You must have known my friend; he was a dance instructor at Ayrshire camp back in the 70s. He was renowned for his patience and abilities to *lead* as he would say. Colin taught the international standard, Latin and social dances such as nightclub two-step and single time swing." Jesus hopped on the spot and did a few Michael Jackson style twirls, to Donald and Edna's amusement. He continued, "Many an accomplished dancer that set foot on a slipperine dusted dance floor, from all around Scotland, had lessons or some trusted advice from Colin," Jesus spoke softly, almost a whisper.

"In fact, though I shouldn't say this, though rumours circulated at the time that Colin trained the one and only Andy Stewart." Edna's face lit up and was more than happy to hear this story. Jesus continued,

"The Gay Gordons, Strip the Willow and the Dashing White Sergeant. Andy would swirl lassies across the floor to the trained expertise of Colin. Now that is special. Can you imagine? A traditional Scottish TV, Radio, Theatre performer of the highest calibre, trained in dance by the one and only Colin McDonald?"

Sparks were flying in her head as Edna intervened with a soft-spoken voice, "Colin McDonald? We knew Colin, if it's the same Colin McDonald. I can vaguely remember him, but there was a dance tutor during our holidays called Colin, that might be him."

"Well, that is a coincidence! I will speak to him later today, and ask if he remembers you and your husband, John. If you went on holiday every year to Ayr, then I am sure you must have met in the ballroom.

"John and Edna Hughes, you said?" Edna silently nodded in reply.

Jesus continued speaking as he turned to face Donald,

"It must be the same Colin McDonald. Don't you think so, Donald?"

Donald suddenly joined the company in this discussion; his mind had been elsewhere; he didn't have too much time to consider anything positive to say or find appropriate words that would suit the occasion.

"Yes, I'm sure it is him," was the best he could muster.

Edna looked confused and wondered if she told the stranger her surname.

"Now how much do we owe you?" said Jesus.

"Oh, let me think for a moment," she tentatively broached the conversation to gain time. She takes notes on a small notepad and murmurs loudly as if adding the items together. "That will be £25, please."

She waits patiently for a response. A reply from either customer, she thought it would suffice.

She smiled and waited for an answer. Jesus broke the silence.

"Excellent, that sounds fine to me. Donald, can you pay Edna for this splendid assortment of goodies, please?"

Donald murmured the word, "Sure," as he checked his trouser pockets.

He soon discovered as he drew two ten-pound notes and one ultra-modern, plastic Scottish £5 note, in a clenched grip in his right hand. The look on his face showed he had allowed for this experience and expected this type of magical deception, as routine and would happen at some point, at any time. All of this is an affirmed route, in his present land of make-believe. He tentatively handed the money to Edna, as her fingers allocated the appropriate buttons on the ageing cash register which opened, and she delicately placed the notes into separate trays and pushed the drawer firmly back into place.

Jesus lifted the large, well-packed carrier back from the countertop and started to make his way towards the door, and to hear the expecting bell chimes again when Edna spoke. "Excuse me!" she intervened just as the chimes were about to be activated once more.

"You have dropped something," she said, pointing to an envelope that lay on the floor near to where they stood.

Edna had walked towards them and bent over hurriedly to pick up the tattered-looking letter container and spoke,

"Does this belong to you, sir?" She forced yet another smile on her bright and friendly face.

Jesus looked at the envelope and his blue eyes emitted a glow that Donald had borne witness to on many occasions during his short journey with him. The eyes of Edna were now smitten by this attachment also. Edna carefully handed the letter to the stranger. He looked and returned the envelope to her.

"It must be for you, Edna," said Jesus. "Your charity's name on it," handing her the white envelope.

She stared attentively at the writing and rightly enough, written in black ink, the words emblazoned firmly on it, a Heart for the Homeless.

"But there is no stamp!" she stated.

"Maybe it fell from a pocket in the suit we have just purchased?"

Edna took hold of the envelope and gave another long look at it.

"Every item goes through a strict series of examinations. We check every pocket, we look for flaws or damage and we have all our donated clothes dry-cleaned before any item is displayed or sold. So, the envelope could never have come from the suit. I'm sure of that."

"Well, on this occasion, I honestly believe that it has. Trust me!" prompted Donald. He added knowing fine well that Jesus had produced another magical surprise. "Why don't you open it?" Donald prompted Edna.

With her slim fingers, Edna pulled the non-glued flap of the envelope upwards and removed a note. A small black metal paper clip held a cheque, which was attached to the small-lined notepaper.

She seemed shy but excited in a subdued way. She read the short note aloud,

"Please use this money to help Glasgow's homeless. Keep up the good work. My best regards, Jonathon Daily."

Edna looked at both strangers as if seeking some form of assistance until Donald spoke.

"How much is the cheque for?" he inquired. He felt he had intervened and possibly shouldn't have.

It was as if she hadn't placed much thought about the money until Donald mentioned this. Her eyes averted to the charitable gift that she held pinched between both thumbs and both forefingers. By raising and keeping the cheque close to her face, and now focused. She stared through an ageing pair of tortoiseshell-rimmed glasses, which magnified both eyes that gave her a frog-like appearance to her small head. The spectacles took place on a brown rope that looped around her neck and would usually swing below her chin and sit patiently on her chest when not used. She read the amount several times and voiced them in silence, yet no words or sounds passed her lips.

Her look went to and from the cheque to the strangers several times before stopping, then facing the strangers she reacted, and yelled and bellowed each word individually,

"Three. Hundred. And. Fifty. Thousand. Pounds." She repeated the amount, "Three. Hundred. And. Fifty. Thousand. Pounds. I cannot believe this, I cannot believe this." She looked dazed but was in a state of euphoria.

"I can," Donald murmured under his breath.

By the intensity of this event, Edna staggered slowly back towards the counter, where her outstretched arm grasped hold of a small, white plastic garden chair, onto which she slid her slender, frail frame. She stared continually at the cheque, then towards both strangers, a gift such as this will make so much difference to the charity, she was thinking. "I need to phone Joan Hogan, our head of operations," she started to chatter like a songbird again.

"We could advertise or have one of those business sites that people put on computers."

"A website!" offered Donald.

"That's it, a website!" she interrupted herself again. "I must give Joan a call to give her this fantastic news."

She left the comfort of the seat to take a few short steps towards the shop phone, which sat wall-mounted to the rear of the counter. She was aware of silence when she heard the chimes of the doorbell activate, that both strangers had left. Her thought and vision returned to the phone.

By placing the black phone to her right ear, she raised her shoulder in an upward direction, managing to clamp the handset in place, a practice she had done on many occasions in the past. Her forefinger sought the buttons required. Little toned-beeps played as she pressed each large silver button dialling the number. She felt ecstatic, yet unmistakably dumbfounded by a significant amount of money she held in her other hand. A look of contentment showed on her face, and she embraced the excitement, of promoting this fabulous news to her colleague. *The charity is going to be safe and survive*, she thought and waited in anticipation for the head of operations for receiving her call. Waiting for another few dull dialling tones to pass, then someone answered.

"Hello," spoke an elderly woman in a reliant, confident manner as Joan Hogan accepted the call.

The Walk

A low-sounding double-click noise was heard as Donald pointed and pressed a button on a remote-entry key fob in the direction of his cab. Both front and back lights flashed several times to confirm this action, and gave further information to the driver that the doors were now open. Jesus was the first to approach the taxi, he opened the back door and laid the purchased items on the floor. Just as Donald was due to enter his cab, Jesus raised his head above the vehicle roof and spoke, "Let us walk, Donald." The door was closed behind him, and both strolled from the cab. A passing parking warden nodded and smiled as if he was standing guard over the vehicle. Maybe he was!

The streets were busy now. Much more traffic was building up, busy people showing no tolerance of others, only a destination was on each one's mind, whether it was heading to an office, a shop, a cafe for a quick latte, or meeting a friend for a catch-up. Some perusing through newspaper headlines as they stood among an impatient crowd, waiting for the traffic lights to turn green. Most, however, were staring at the screen of their Android phone. Lost in a world of complexity and secrets, not aware of the world around them, as they read and typed messages, sending them to some informative cloud on a super-highway. All personal data held in a matrix of bytes and yottabytes that were deposited in some remote database, somewhere in California's global centre for high-technology Silicon Valley where the world's Techno knowledge is caught, and collated and held.

High-tech, modern science showed much confusion to many on-lookers similar in mind to Donald. Social media is now part of the daily ritual rather than making a simple chat with each other, which used to be very much apart from the human condition. Technologically illiterate passers-by could only imagine what nature of information people would be continually sending on their mobile handsets. (The weather is miserable again. My train has been delayed; seemingly wet leaves are stuck on the track. I have an early morning meeting with the CEO. It took me hours to type out a large data file last night. Do you still work on Ingram Street? How about lunch? Let's organise a night out!)

Most people nowadays are on the worldwide computer network of a digital social grid. Typing text that placed their brief private broadcast on a personal virtual timeline. While significantly critiquing others for inappropriate comments, though they still believe wholeheartedly in their self-importance. A selfie of a dour face woman stuck in traffic on a packed city bus hits her web-based profile with the headlines: "More delays and sense more misery in this dull crappy day." Wondered how many comments and 'likes' she will receive as she stares at the phone hopeful of likeable reviews or comments.

Those days of honest and personal communication are no longer with us. Never had Donald viewed or examined the human psyche up, close and so personal. It was all new to him. He was not out and about, and amongst them, or part of the crowd. Going with the flow, as he imagined.

A few tourists and some city guests had gathered in a small group at the equestrian statue of the Duke of Wellington which sat in a prominent position in Royal Exchange Square. The world-famous, 'Jock of Wellington', the hero with a red and white traffic cone stuck on his head. Many corporate leaders and distinguished folk of Glasgow fought many a battle in a hope to stop this unacceptable Vandalism and continual damage caused by this aggressive action, to such a unique bronze design by the notable Italian sculptor, Baron Carlo Marochetti, in the mid-19th century.

"So, what do you think of the statue, Donald? Is it better with the cone or without?" spoke Jesus as they both stepped close to the plinth of the statue and stood among many people who took photographs with either a phone or an expensive camera with all sorts of contraptions added to it. A lens or lenses with filters gave it a more professional look.

"I love it! People expect to see it like this." He smiled and looked at Jesus and added, "I think it's cool!"

"So, do I, I am a fan of Jock of Wellington too. Let's get a few photographs."

Donald pulled his mobile phone from his jacket and did likewise with his glasses. He gazed carefully at the screen of the mobile, looked for a small image of a camera lens that would prove to be the tool he required. After locating the camera app, his finger pressed the button. *A pleased Jesus in Glasgow and on the road with me,* he thought this unbelievable.

Now, this is a wonder!

The day was beautiful, and the sky was cloudless for this winter day. Even warm in comparison to recent weather, or as most television meteorologists would commonly offer: "As far back as records go."

The city was in good cheer.

The Meet

A group of four people raced in haste and soon arrived at the charity shop; they had used numerous forms of transportation of their individual choice to get there to the little charity shop as Edna Hughes had waited in trepidation for their arrival. The atmosphere inside the gift shop was highlighted by an air of richness, as they absorbed the recent bonanza. An original form of comfort enveloped them in such a positive manner with grace and cheerfulness, as they felt thankful for such a gift from this mysterious, big-hearted donor.

Edna handed the cheque to Joan who in turn had discussed the provenance and real possibilities of the donation; with Hector Ford, the solicitor, charged with the charities overall business and legal duties.

His expected phone call from their bank made the team freeze, as they stood in silence, hoping, wishing, praying as expectation crept through them all, as he listened intently to the deep-toned voice emanated from the receiver. He nodded frequently, thanked the caller and did not return any questions, he offered his thanks then switched his mobile off. Not a giveaway sign appeared on his face and no one could read his look as he placed his phone into his pocket before he ran both hands through his bay rum scented grey hair then entwined both in a tightly tensioned grip on the nape of his neck. He spoke, "It's all above board. It is 100% legal. The cheque is real and for our charity. All of it!"

They cheered and laughed, gave hugs to each other to make a day more special than any other day. A time to make plans. More money to help the homeless.

"I'll nip out for a bottle or two of bubbly. We need to celebrate this fantastic news," said Jim Malcolm, also a director and fundraiser for the charity He spluttered a few illegible words that no one heard before he left the shop, in his search for a nearby off-licence.

Shona Turtle, another executive, though a well-known soft and timid-hearted person, a spinster of several years, stood a step or two back from the group as her fingertips smothered her lips. Her eyes, however, showed the smile her mouth didn't, and most delightfully, she danced as if a butterfly moved between flower heads in a garden filled with nectar. Later, and a few sips too many of sparkly Italian wine, would have her giggle spasmodically at every phrase or sentence her tipsy colleagues spoke. The delight of today's windfall would last with them all into the early hours, with many new plans being thrashed out over more and more drinks. They would discuss how this vast amount of money could help the charity, possibly purchase a van to gather new stock, have additional staff, promotion through a website with an online shop, upgrade their image and branding, make sure the brand looks purposeful and acceptable for all age groups. The staff were full of ideas, ideas that are better served sober when brainstorming could be discussed then agreed, possibly over a hot breakfast. Eventually, after a few more bottles of wine were consumed, they added more proposals to the ever increased and enlarged scheme, all designed for the charities rebirth.

"Let's take this fabulous gift and use it to capitalise better days to come. To our precious gift!" shouted Shona but fumbled a few words due to her intoxication, she stood unsteadily on her feet and raised her glass to the humour of the company. She fell backwards but, luckily, caught before a full table of drinks were splattered, as she was gently assisted to her seat. Though she couldn't hear the further conversation, she smiled and nodded her head to the rhythmic beat of the chit-chat, tried hard to look sober and compos mentis. Her head bobbed around her neck and shoulders as an egg did in a pot of boiled water.

The next day would spin out with more excitement, fun and laughter; the day was joyful, the day got busy, in fact, more energetic than ever in the small charity shop history. Without carrying forwards any of the plans discussed over many drinks, the shop got busy without any help whatsoever. It was strange. The charity shop suddenly became the place to shop, the place to be. Mentioned on social media as the place to buy fabulous clothes. The coolest of all charity shops! Customers came and went. Merchandised bags full of recently purchased goods. The clothing racks didn't swell or bevel as they once did, the items were selling like hot cakes. The shelves looked light of products. They need more stock! What *a day it's been,* Edna happily thought. *What another day it's been!*

The Gathering

"What about some music, Donald?" said Jesus as they walked from the Royal Exchange square towards Buchannan Street.

As Donald followed Jesus, a voice entered his mind and narrated the following words:

This is particle intervention.

Either a coincidental assembly, a pre-arranged meeting, or a general crossing of paths, or a day when everyone wants to do the same thing. This random connection is called particle intervention, which is a law that straightforwardly governs all life.

Now, this law requires a spark or someone to ignite the project. A thought could do it, a word or a scream might kick-start an event, an uncoordinated meeting, or in the final moment of an abhorrent misfortune may divulge the countdown to it all beginning. An assembly of two people and their future family may be the start of something way beyond belief!

Take Mahatma Gandhi as an example of this phenomena. His father, Karamchand Gandhi, married four times. His first two wives died young, and each marriage produced a daughter, and his third marriage was childless.

In 1857, Karamchand, after his third wife's consent to remarry; he wed a young woman called Putlibai. Karamchand and Putlibai had three children over the next decade, two sons, Laxmidas and Karsandas, and, a daughter, Raliatbehn.

On 2nd October 1869, Putlibai gave birth to her last child, Mohandas, in a ground-floor room of the Gandhi family home in Porbandar. Through all this particle intervention, and years of complicated family trials and tribulations, the result of all of this is Mahatma Gandhi. A pure, white glowing, radiant soul who spread love and compassion to all.

Though this may not be a perfect or a relevant example, it should at least let you understand how this law works in its purest form. Just say a person ventured out from a five-storey window, intent on jumping. People will watch with an inquisitive, yet distressed curiosity. To view with intrigue a person balanced on a small, yet delicate window ledge and invite other passers-by to join them. As momentum builds and as anxiety grows, the crowd inhale a ghoulish enthusiasm to be active and participate to see some poor soul lost within the human condition, place the final moments of a struggled life at the mercy of others. All eyes stared at the jumper's tensioned fingers and white knuckles that bulged in pain, as the jumper clutches at any suitable hold the window and frame collectively offer; before he jumps or not. Then the herd of gruesome viewers inclusively react with short breath screams as they observe a few loose pieces of mortar chips crumble beneath the jumper's foothold. As fragments of stone plummet ground ward, it gives the prime candidate a glimpse of what will come next.

But why hold on? If the window jumper is determined to go head first, then why create an audience? Just jump!

The law is simple in its complexity; it becomes an instant attraction which gathers structure fast.

It doesn't sound much like a particle code event or anywhere near it, but it does attract a crowd and will always remain part of that law. It still does. Just imagine an intense fire in a tenement where troubled people are seen at every window screaming for help or see police officers chasing drug-fuelled shoplifters. Crowds will gather to watch and discuss these situations. Do they seek information? Do they feel they need to bear witness?

All these parts are within the realms of 'particle intervention'. It is the attraction this or that, which doesn't seem to be part of the standard day to day activities you experience. You accept the level as, well, a benchmark. It is everywhere. OK, I don't want to make this further complicated than it already is, but particle intervention in the context of life, in general, happens to everyone. It happens to all animals, all creatures of the sea, insects and plants, planets and stars, cosmos and universe, this and that, topsy-turvy, etc. It's a law of laws and proposals of laws within statutes.

OK, it's when many people gather to enjoy a moment in time when all in their immediate vicinity are caught and drawn into a shared magical moment of the governing law, or in the eye of the hurricane would describe it correctly.

Here is a notable example.

The voice disappeared.

Buchannan Street was busy with Xmas shoppers. Business people were doing lunch in trendy coffee houses, most showed a fixed or vacant expression as they stood in a chaotic queue to wait for service and gave a long stare at the wall menu before being served. Some had already decided their choice and ordered their personal favourite coffee; some would order a large vanilla latte with a veggie ciabatta, a cafe mocha with a double shot for the stressed executive, a flat white and scrambled-egg croissant, sprinkled with flaky salt and chopped chives for the healthy minded financier. One person sat in the window seat and read the *Herald,* and consumed a buttered-scone and drank a small Con Panna with a bottle of Scottish still water as an accompaniment. The fashion provocateur wore an Ermenegildo Zegna suit demonstrated his imaginary hold on success, he drank from a glass cup that held dark Cafe Americano which, he thought, added to his style and quality. A large wall poster depicted a white mug of hot coffee showed a slogan attached said: *Depresso, the feeling you get when you run out of coffee.*

Tourists took photographs of old Victorian buildings most Glaswegians never fully noticed or even paid any attention to. Pensioners were window shopping and collected the few last presents for Xmas, students looked for bargains and general offers or possibly stocking fillers for classmates, teenagers want the latest mobile phone and money's best tablet that brought extra power to portability and to give a higher social acceptance to their peers. Smaller children pulled the arms of their mothers, attempted to attract them to the shop with the magical toy window display. Parents and children alike stood and stared in amazement at the best window display in Glasgow. Artificial snow had been attached to the glass and covered most of the scene; the main backdrop presented a festive country cottage winter scene which revealed the house fully lit and warm, there was an enormous decorated tree that illuminated one side of the window. The main observation was a large sleigh, one life-size toy reindeer with a red nose that flashed, and a mixture of toy elves filled the remaining window space. A mountain of Xmas wrapped boxes and presents smothered the scene. A hefty pot-bellied Santa sat prominently on the sleigh and his remotely controlled large gloved hand continually waved towards the public, a tape loop of ho-ho-ho sounded loud and cheerful as customers entered the shop. A big neon sign swung above the sleigh and said, 'Merry Xmas Glasgow'.

Just as Jesus and Donald entered Buchannan Street, Jesus offered Donald a spectacle case which looked old and tattered. "Try these glasses on, Donald," said Jesus in a hopeful way.

Though not too sure what the purpose of these glasses meant, he looked at Jesus keenly and took the case in his hand, opened it to reveal a small, round-lensed pair of glasses that did not give any appearance to value or quality.

"They look like John Lennon's glasses," offered Donald as the only words he could grasp.

"Mohandas Karamchand Gandhi wore these glasses for many years," said Jesus. As he observed, Donald thoroughly inspected the glasses.

"Wow, Gandhi! They are special, but they feel fragile and antiquated. I don't want to damage something so historical and unique," said Donald as he studied the glasses further.

"Try them on. You will see the benefits of such special lenses.

"Round glasses are worn by enlightened people you will know as Gandhi and as you mentioned; John Lennon."

Donald carefully placed the spectacle case into his pocket then stretched the steel temple arms over his ears as the frame held tight against his nose. He adjusted the eyeglasses slightly then looked at Jesus. He felt joyous and elevated at how he saw him. "All I see is pure white light nearby you. Is it an aura? It is glorious!" He turned his head to look at many people nearby, hoping to see an aura of a generated bright light emanating from each of them.

"What do you see, Donald?" Jesus questioned him.

"There are many colours. I don't understand. Every colour I could imagine being emitted and radiated from the people. All ages and sizes but so many different colours, on so many people." Donald removed the glasses as he felt unable to comprehend the significance of the phenomenon, he just has borne witness.

"Is this how we all look?" He continued, "If we all emit different colours, then why don't we know which colour we are, what does it all mean?" He looked for answers; he searched for the truth. He just observed a miracle, a miracle that possibly Gandhi had access to over a century before.

Jesus answered, "The rainbow colours are disciplines given to every individual born soul in every being that has lived or will ever live. All humans and creatures alike are born with a white inner glow. It is how an individual spends their life that will ultimately determine their fate: right or wrong, yin or yang. It is the triumph of good over evil. There is always a choice in life. The goodness of heart emanates from a soul full of joy and giving. Though you must remember, darkness can overwhelm a lost soul who has wandered from the flock. Spirits can fall into darkness, a blackness that will hold them in a tightly held grasp, and keep them feckless and dissolute in any life they may have left on this earth. There is, however, an all-powerful substance that conquers all. It is the easiest, the most abundant element in all creation. One that can't be measured or viewed under a microscope; it's invisible to all that search for it but easy to find. And that most powerful of God's creation, is love!"

Carefully, Donald listened as Jesus continued, "Love is the cleanser, love is the elixir, love is the hope, love is the truth, love is everything. Love is God."

"Did Gandhi see coloured auras?" was his choice of question.

"Yes. With good and bad observance. Gandhi observed many dark colours among people he would trust and call friends, yet he never disowned them or had them leave his company. He offered love in return. Only love."

"Did he see a dark aura when his killer walked towards him?" Donald enquired.

"As did John Lennon. Both men saw their killers' approach; both Gandhi and Lennon knew the evil that lay within each of the tarnished souls of both assassins, as evil loomed to terminate each of their lives. They accepted a fate both believed ran through their different lives. In John's life, he realised from an early age, that the number 9 would be a fixture in his days on earth. It would make him who he was, and help him decide and develop a future he could take forwards with this number being a significant factor in all his trials and tribulations, from the start of his life to his last day on earth.

"His birthday was the 9th October, the first house he lived in was 9, Newcastle Road, the Beatles first appearance in the Cavern Club was February 9th, 1961 and his second son, Sean, was born on the 9th October 1975. It included songs such as Revolution 9 and #9Dream among many other coincidences followed John until the day he died. Which was the 8th of December 1980 New York time, but in his place of birth, Liverpool, it was the 9th.

"He knew his future. He saw his life through those round glasses.

"While John spent time in Rishikesh, India, with his fellow Beatles in February 1968, a guru had observed John as a man of vision, and he presented the glasses to him. John Lennon knew too well that all teachers were once pupils, so learning was the way to understand the truth. He once said, 'All I want is the truth, just give me some truth.'

"John Lennon knew that all truth begins with knowledge of spirituality. He spoke of the universe, peace, love, truth, God or imagine a place where all human beings lived as one. And through all his efforts, became a leader to millions of people in modern culture. In his time, he had followers that believed his words.

"He sang *Give Peace a Chance*, where he offered his peaceful thoughts through music and lyrics. So that love would prevail."

"Didn't he once say he was bigger than Jesus, sorry; bigger than you?" said Donald in an inquisitive voice.

"He said, The Beatles were more popular than Jesus. Religious beliefs change daily, and if anyone could encourage views through peaceful acts such as John Lennon did, to millions of followers, then I'm all in favour. He was a kind-hearted soul," Jesus added.

"Each soul must recognise the experience when they arrive at the truth," he finished speaking.

Jesus walked into the heart of Buchannan Street; Donald lagged somewhat behind.

In an unexpected moment, a deluge of rain, a mini monsoon in biblical terms poured relentlessly down on Buchannan Street and drenched many of its occupants. This sudden micro-climate soaked everyone as people scurried for the cover of many shaped, brand-promoted canopies, shop fronts or protection inside the nearest shop, cafe or pub. However, it lasted only a few seconds. The storm passed, and it stopped, it left behind overflowed drains that sucked gallons of flood water into the depths of an overwhelmed drainage system. Puddles formed and lay around the paved street that proved there had been a significant rainstorm of some kind. Soaked to the skin, many people remained in the comfort of a heated shop. Some stood near winter convectors, which blasted out welcomed air, within its process, would hopefully help dry their clothes.

Many onlookers stared skyward, and were amazed to see a bright and cloudless clear sky and were awestruck by the sudden changes to the weather.

Not a rain cloud or any potential severe weather approaching. The sky looked as perfect as it did minutes before. It must have been a freak of nature.

The street got busy again as people ventured out and about, and got back to the daily routine, by filling the streets.

Did Jesus perform this rain burst miracle? Donald thought this but did not ask.

As Jesus and Donald approached the junction of Gordon Street and Buchannan Street, a busker started to set up his equipment in a central position, close by TGI Fridays. A spark of spontaneous combustion was at work as fellow musicians approached his pitch and began to add their musical material to the stack which grew by the second. A cellist sat on a small foldable chair and proceeded to tune the strings, while a bass player and his two friends plugged electric guitar leads micro amplifiers. A violinist waited for instructions. A stout keyboard player unpacked his kit and prepared his vocal microphone which gave a few high-pitched whistles. A drummer took his equipment from a makeshift trolley and was ready to play in under a minute, a bagpipe player, perched on wooden stilts, stood over eight feet in height, approached the melee ready and eager to participate. Acoustic guitarists came from all directions and merged into the ensemble of performers. Carol singers joined the increased crowd. A sax player ran through the musical scales and had acceded to a group of twenty other musicians of all sorts of talent and ambition. His fingerless gloves matched the grey woollen hat that covered most of his longish blonde hair.

Now, a group of pedestrians had started to form in a congregation around the assembled entertainers, all ready to participate in whatever song was about to begin. People were prepared to accept the situation and be part of it.

The instigator of this event made a few brief expressions to his fellow musicians as his electric guitar swung readily from his shoulder. He nodded at the drummer, who in turn hit a drumstick against the rim of the snare as the initial count to start the song.

The busker opened the song with a loud amplified vocal that began to reverberate through every ear over a long distance within reach of the city centre. Fellow musicians started to play the song as if they had worked together for years, all in tune and perfect time. He sang Glasgow band, Travis, classic 1999 song, *Why does it always rain on me,* which was very appropriate for the occasion and very cheeky Glasgow in style. His voice threw out the first few lines while nearly every other person in attendance joined in on the mass karaoke; a Glasgow collective. He continued to sing about sunny days, and where they had gone?

More and more people joined the massed crowd, and a few more musicians joined the merry band of troubadours. All played with one voice and one beating heart.

As the lead vocalist started the chorus, nearly all the people on Buchannan Street were involved in one way or the other; the energy was infectious, even police officers joined a group of girls on a hen party and danced near the musicians. The street came to life as dancing and singing broke out in every corner. People of all ages got involved. A street sweeper partnered his brush on a slow foxtrot; a few beggars had made their way into the group, and joined the festivities and applauded this massive effort. A mass of voices enveloped the street as the chorus started:

The main singer asked a question on why does it always rain on him, and wanted to know if it was because he lied when he was seventeen.

Everyone knew the lyrics. All joined in with the mass choral extravaganza.

They sang their collective hearts out!

Two women approached the gathering and started to applaud the energy of all who participated in the musical process. A senior man, dressed finely and wore a black suit with well-polished black brogues on his feet, a crisp white shirt adorned with a bright purple tie, which made him stick out from the crowd; offered his hand to one of the two women. "Would you like to dance?" Although slightly, and far from her comfort zone, though a few gentle hints and shoulder nudges from her friend, she accepted. Both Edna and her dance companion joined many people as they danced to the organic sound that drifted around the city centre. Photographs and videos landed on social media sites, and one video would reach a worldwide audience with over two million views before the New Year arrived.

The chorus instigated another full response. With everyone joining in. Once again singing why rain fell on him, and if it was because he lied when he was a teenager. But sing they did, and everyone sang the Travis song beautifully. A rendition the band would surely be proud of!

Even when the sun is shining, I can't avoid the lightning.
More and more dance groups broke out along Buchannan Street, couples danced with their partners, friends with friends and strangers danced with strangers. As the song tapered to a finale, the applause was deafening. Cheers reverberated up and down the full length of the street and the many roads that adjoined it. It was a mega burst of joy, as one person said. Telephone numbers and email addresses passed between those that had met at the gathering. Some gave cuddles and kisses, some patted backs, and proper smiles decorated the neighbourhood as never seen before. A young man chatted with a young woman he had performed in a group dance, and with no previous conviction or confidence, bravely asked if she would like to join him for lunch at a nearby cafe. The cafe, which he nodded his head in the direction of, or she had assumed, and where the eatery stood. She agreed.

As the group dispersed slowly, the mood was still highly charged with love and hope. *Glasgow smiles better,* many people thought. *What a way to spend a day and such a great honour to have been a part of this phenomena.*

The old dancer returned his partner to where her friend stood and where she had enjoyed the spectacle; she had smiled and laughed and participated fully in the experience. "Wow, how fantastic were you, Edna, I didn't know you could dance like that," she said, as she threw her arms around her neck and gave a long tight hug.

"She is delightful, my dear. Very light on her feet and certainly a joy to dance with," said the old gent whose face turned red with his recent physical struggles.

"I haven't enjoyed myself for many a day. I didn't believe I could dance as well as this as it's been so long since I moved so energetically," said Edna holding her hand and proposed a handshake, which the old man approved with an exceptional, robust and trustworthy grip.

"You are more than welcome. Maybe we can meet again? I run a dance club at a local school near where I live. The club always needs new members. Especially ones that can dance as good as you."

"I'm not sure. I don't know if I could find the time. Let me think about it," Edna responded unassured and in an apprehensive way.

The old man took a business card from his inside pocket. "Here's my card, and if you fancy a night of dance moves with an old charmer like myself, then you won't beat my class. Just remember, life isn't waiting for the storm to pass, it's about learning to dance in the rain," he said joyfully.

Edna took his card and just as she was about to put it into her open handbag, she stopped and stared at the business call card. Froze slightly, then stared at the stranger.

"Is there something wrong?" he replied.

"Are you Colin McDonald that instructed dance classes at Butlin's way back in the 70s?" Edna strained her eyes towards the senior man.

She waited eagerly for a positive response.

Edna's face lit up, she was a young school girl again, she hoped and prayed that this is the man from her past, the man she had recently discussed at length with two strangers in the charity shop.

"I am, yes. Do we know each other?" Colin was slightly mystified but pleasantly optimistic about the question. His last few days had been strange also. He had met someone from his past that instantly encouraged him to get out and do more. Not just run a weekly dance class. Do more! Respond to new people, use social skills that he once held in abundance and was famed. Use the talent he was born with to enlighten others. If it meant dance lessons were to be taught, to others less capable, then he should promote his class and open it up to a broader audience. Allow more people to enjoy the natural blend of music and dance he loved since he was a boy. Share a mutual goal was the sentence he remembered.

Even being advised and encouraged to look at work options, for a man of his age, job hunting was not a task he felt comfortable with. *What job can a man my age do?* He did realise, however, that still fit and active for his years, a small part-time job could have benefits, and not just financial ones. It would get him out of the house more often and give him a chance to achieve more, which in turn, would give him a dependable and friendly social future. He held excellent leadership abilities and stronger communication skills than the younger generation. Give it a go! Why not?

He could still show the younger generation a thing or two.

Stacking shelves at the local DIY store were not to his liking, nor to move an item passed a barcode scanner did not make a notable attraction to him either. Maybe something agreeable would raise its ugly head and present a job suited to an older adult. He was up for the challenge if the right situation came around.

Just as Edna was about to chirp like a little songbird once more, her face showed delight when the old man responded, "Yes, I worked many seasons at Ayr. Can you remember me by my name? I have changed a little." He laughed.

As Edna was about to enlist the help of her newly recalled memories, memories of her magical times at Ayr Butlin's, the arrival of Jesus and Donald managed to stop her mid-sentence. She looked towards the two men and spoke.

"Mighty me! Just as I was about to explain my story to you, Colin, these two gentlemen turn up. How strange can this day be?" she continued. "These are the two remarkable men that mentioned you, Colin, and if it weren't for meeting them today, our charity would never have discovered the gift we always prayed and wished." Edna smiled as Colin took a step closer to Jesus.

"Ah, my friend, how are you?" said Colin as he looked towards Jesus and took his hand, held it tightly and shook it firmly.

Donald's face looked puzzled, it seemed strained, and he was lost for words as his mind offered only a few dubious answers to some of the infinite amounts of questions still swirled around inside his numb and incessant conscious thoughts, he knew only Jesus could answer. *Mainly, when did the old man receive the bags of clothes? The bags were in my taxi for over an hour or so? Do Colin and Edna see a different Jesus from me? If he met Colin at Ayr in the 1970s, then he must look older. He must look different. At least, not like the Jesus I see. Not one thing makes sense!*

Colin, in a bright, uplifted voice spoke,

"It was nice to meet this morning, and of course, I must thank you for the kind gifts. My only other suit has seen better days that's for sure and this gift is just delightful." The elderly man added, "Today, I feel young again, and I thank you kindly for all you have done."

The Flight

Once again and in a split moment of magic, Donald and Jesus left the conversation and the environment of solid ground of Buchannan Street behind, only to discover each floated a few hundred feet above the city. Donald's first reaction was to feel fear, but his body felt relaxed, and his companion was undoubtedly the ablest and most trustworthy aerial ally. He studied the city below. "Do they know we have just left them, and can they see us up here?" he said as he bobbed in the form of microgravity. Not behold to gravity or torn away towards the moon or even further afield, but stationary, yet he could roll and move as smooth as if in a warm pool of water. He enjoyed this.

"No, they didn't know we were there. Edna, Shona and Colin were drawn to the wonder of the party because they have pure souls. The enjoyment was for all that participated. Particle intervention makes every individual the creator of their reality. It is their choice to go one way or the other. I just helped with some parts of it today," he added. "Try the glasses on, Donald."

A quick fumble in his jacket pocket brought the spectacle receptacle into view, he struggled as if he didn't want to drop them, but happily realised that this would not happen. He returned the case to his pocket then twisted the glasses into place over his nose and adjusted the frame slightly as he stared below at what remained of the still overly enthusiastic crowd.

"Most of the people I see are radiant white!" he enthusiastically uttered. "I can't see any colours," he concluded.

Jesus stared at Donald and gave a warm smile. "Not all dark-coloured auras are sick or unfortunate souls. Many characters you saw earlier could have been associated with that person going through a bad patch. Possibly going through a divorce, move to a new house, conflict at work, money problems, health issues, having lost a loved one or a dear friend, miss a beloved pet, a favourite football team lost an important match or numerous amounts of affiliated sources, all of which can darken a spirit. I quote a young woman from history, Anne Frank, 'No one becomes poor by giving.'"

Both moved off in a gentle motion upward and further across the city, they soared like a Chinese dragon kite, rotated through low clouds and swooped through the pressure of air with effortless grace. He was free as a bird and content in doing so. He flew happily through the sky and was drawn as metal to a magnet by the free-flowed movement made by Jesus. He felt like a passenger in the world's best roller coaster.

He saw Glasgow as only a bird or insect would see. A drone could have a view like this. He observed the taxi rank near Queen Street railway station where he would usually tout for business, and a traffic warden still gave grief to drivers attempting to enter and join a full queue of parked cars. They drove their taxis a few circuits around the block and hoped that space became available, this was always the preferred option which would hopefully ward off the over-zealous warden bent on sticking a ticket under a window wiper.

Donald kept his stare in the nearby German Market below as it took prominence in George Square. He thought the most enchanting thing about German Christmas markets is all the little things that never change. Children gathered around the nativity scene which was sheltered under a canopy. Adults wrapped up in warm clothes clustered near the Glühwein stalls and drank hot mulled wine with added cinnamon or vanilla, a sweet-smell aroma from spicy bratwurst sausages, schnitzel and ham and crackling and pork rolls to ridiculously cheesy covered garlic bread and warm gingerbread bouquets fanned through the air. Carols were heard from a small group of singers. Many shoppers come here to stock up on gifts and delicacies at many stalls sold wintery treats, and arts and crafts. Locals often visit for a few drinks and a bite to eat. You can't help thinking this is how Xmas used to be, and how it ought to be. Donald needs to get Xmas back into his life again, as he flew off in another direction and away from the area.

The Theatre

A peaceful silence gave sanctuary to Donald's thoughts as his feet touched gingerly down on a construction roof he didn't immediately recognise. He looked around and hoped to achieve a bearing on his location. And as he looked street ward, he soon understood and knew where his feet had landed.

"We are in the Trongate," he said in a sure way to himself, stood lightly, yet safely, on the edge of the roof of the Panopticon Theatre.

"There is something special I want you to see, Donald," Jesus said, and placed a hand on Donald's shoulder, they left the space of the grey slate roof and miraculously appeared in the wings, near the stage of a busy working theatre.

It was smoky, warm and smelled of many collected odours he couldn't identify, and he felt the tension of a very hostile environment that lurked somewhere in the darkness of the stalls.

Donald's curiosity took hold when he held back part of the red velvet curtain which swung with weight at the side of the stage where he stood, to view a scurrilous audience of rough and ready characters, guzzling copious quantities of what he assumed was bottled alcohol. Others devoured what looked like mince or mutton pies, which showed significant amounts of grease dripping from them. He saw enormous gas-lit chandeliers firmly suspended from high in the auditorium ceiling, which illuminated the vaulted area, but not much of the central light source brightened the floor level where he could only view the first few rows of seats where the angry crowd punished the stage performers to their amusement.

The inebriated audience participated together in a shared habit by following influences of a certain few loudmouths, which encouraged like-minded people to do the same. Those angry voices threw defamatory abuse at a young man as he stood alone on centre stage. Items such as horse manure, nails, stones, rivets and rotten fruit and vegetables littered the floor around the young fellow who was brave enough to venture on stage and practise his newfound trade with hope to entertain, one of Britain's most unforgiving audiences.

Some clumps of rotten vegetables were stuck hard to the bright hot limelight's that lit the front of the performance area. Predictably, this would enhance a more repulsive stink to the arena. The young man struggled in earnest to complete his act had much abuse rained down upon him, along with all sorts of missiles that mostly found their target. One projectile in question had hit the bull's eye, which led to a vigorous and over-zealous cheer from a hostile and impatient crowd.

A lucky, yet precisely thrown tomato managed to knock the ill-fitting, tattered top hat that sat precariously on the young man's head, which caused it to tumble onto the stage near his feet. More and more belly laughs ensued to the young comic's downfall rather than feed his over-eager first attempt to be successful at an amateur theatre night. The Glasgow crowd was well-known for its hard-hitting demeanour, but he took all of this in his stride as he battled through torrents of abuse to complete his performance. As he bent over to pick up his hat, a well-timed jocular trip managed to set his right foot forwards, so it launched the headwear off the stage and into the orchestra pit below which now raised laughs for his act, and not at his demise they earlier desired. The crowd suddenly realised that this young man could make them laugh and gave amusement to a few hecklers who applauded his venture and nerve. He now threw some of his best jokes in a rapid presentation in a hope to hold onto this newly found route to glory. "What is the difference between a tube and a foolish Dutchman? One is a hollow cylinder and the other a silly Hollander," he asked and answered his joke instantaneously. A few giggles bellowed among the residual hecklers that continued to interact with the entertainers. "I have a large book of jokes at home – I wished I had here it with me." A few more laughs gave the audience a view that the young man tried his very best and many of the audience showed their appreciation. His time on stage ended as the compare offered the audience applause to Arthur Jefferson for his genuine effort.

However, as he completed his act, Arthur walked off stage to a broad mix of ridicule and praise; his first ever performance was over, yet he managed to slide on a pre-placed banana skin and struggled to find the balance of this newfound routine where he tried to stay upright. But to no avail, as his slender frame crash landed entirely on his backside. This last piece of action gave more laughs and additional confidence to his first attempt at being a music hall comedian. After all, he was a month short of his 16th birthday. He approached the wing where both Jesus and Donald stood, pulled a clean handkerchief from his trouser pocket, and wiped the sweat and other gunk from his face which also removed most of the black grease paint that had been carefully applied an hour or so, previously. He stopped at once where they had viewed his performance and turned to stare in their direction. Though the young comedian could not see them, it was as if there he had a feeling that someone, or a presence was there – a sense of being watched. He looked in that direction for a moment then continued onward, he walked down several steps, and along a darkly lit corridor towards the small shared dressing room, he inhabited with other amateur acts.

As they followed the young man to the dressing room, they heard more hostilities from the stage, as a well-spoken, loud voice of a lean, skeletal-type dandy dressed compare, announce yet another victim, to expectantly entertain the gathered madness. Once again, raised voices and a splatter of vegetables could be heard hitting the floor as a young woman attempted to sing *Ta-Ra-Ra Boom-de-ay* at the top of her angelic toned voice. The small orchestra shared her attempted avoidance of spoilt fruit and vegetable rain falls, as it landed in bundles of horrendous filth towards them, made individual musicians miss some notes as they ducked and dived for cover. But being professional, they played with the hope of finishing the show. The show must go on!

The young comedian was overwhelmed by his first ever experience to perform to an audience. He had the bug: the smells, the atmosphere, the ambience and the strange theatrical characters he met on this excursion to become professional. The abuse forced upon him, the fellow entertainers he met backstage would all be a dominant source of learning which he would later rely on, a place of make-believe where he could always be someone else. All of this would set him up for his future endeavours. Tonight's escapade refreshed something in him, a drug of sorts, he had at last found his calling. "This professional theatre life is the way forwards," he muttered to himself as he entered the small dusky dressing room.

The room had a table backed by a large, square black spot covered mirror that showed little perfection on any visible reflection, which would be necessary for its intended use. One overheated wall lamp that barely lit the room, far less assist the acts in preparation for their show. It burned a slow continuous blue flame, accompanied by a sparking noise from the fiery glow the light produced. A few church size candles added a much-needed brightness to the dark room which then threw scattered light upon the walls, which illuminated a multitude of promotional items attached. One wall was covered by marketing or self-promotional literature.

The fantastic Waldo Fenn, the snake man, was classed as the best contortionist in the business. The Mountain Giant from Egypt stood over 12 feet tall and would wrestle any three hopefuls that wished to challenge him. Violet Bloom, a mezzo-soprano songbird, who had performed for most of Europe's Royalty and aristocratic blue-bloods in most major continental cities. The Snarkle Trio was a group of musicians from Edinburgh and had been regulars on the circuit throughout Scotland for many years. And the Corsican pirates, a group of acrobats that performed remarkable feats of balance on high wires. One of their troupe, Antone Francescu, would set a large wooden tub, filled with water, spin at the top of a long pole. Then roamed around the stage for over a minute or so, he would wait for the agreed timed sound of a snare drum roll to stop. He would whip the pole away to gasps from the audience, and the container would drop over seven metres and hurtle towards him. He would hope to catch the tub on the spike of a helmet he had tightly strapped to his head. If misjudged, the centre by a couple of centimetres, the impact would throw him across the stage. Or cause severe damage to his health.

The flying trapeze man artwork showed a lithograph of him airborne at a great height. A worn reproduction piece of promotional material that looked seriously water damaged, discoloured and faded at the edges. All the way from Russia, the print stated. With synonyms such as bold, courageous, audacious, adventurous, venturesome and fearless. All words used indiscriminately and covered most of the large poster that hung insecurely on the wall which should depict him as the World's best high-wire act.

Sultan Bin Ali Bacca and his flying carpet showed him dressed in an ankle length white thawb and full Ottoman's sultan turban. He was an Italian citizen from Naples as it explicitly mentioned as a footnote: Luigi Esposito from Naples will appear as Sultan bin Ali Bacca a classical mind-reading act.

The Swanson swells, these character singers dressed as fashionable, flashy young men and sang songs about high life and drank generous amounts of champagne. Their unfashionable songs boasted about being idle, drunk and forever associated with women. To be seen at the most popular places, their attitude was distinctly laddish. They were popular with the ladies, as boy bands are today.

Also nailed to the wall were a multitude of business cards or self-promoting literature. An extensive and varied selection of artists, agents, hoteliers, stage suppliers, technicians and many with theatre trade connections had left their mark. The young performer was still on cloud nine with his first effort to perform before an audience. He slumped his slender frame onto the empty chair that sat opposite another young amateur comedian who had entertained the audience an hour or so ago, he offered a few words, "You did well, Stanley. I was amazed at how you turned your act around. It was so much funnier than my routine."

Stanley picked up a bottle of beer, lit a cigarette that swung from his lower lip, from one of the large candles that sat near him, inhaled the great, non-filtered smoke and coughed several times before clearing his throat. "I think you were beautiful, William," he said as he drank a mouthful of warm beer.

"No, I have done what I always wanted to do, and one attempt on stage is more than enough. I can be funny on the streets, joke with friends, but up there, on stage and in front of bloodthirsty pagans is something I don't want to sample again. I have lived my dream thankfully. I just needed to try the stage one time only and I have done that. You, however, are like a sponge. You soaked up and absorbed every facet of the occasion. It is you that is meant to be doing this, Stanley. Only you!" said William as he drank beer from the small brown bottle, he had cupped in his hands.

"It invigorates me, William. I feel fresh and renewed. It is as lightning has struck me and the experience performing on stage charges me with lots of energy. It's a drug I will always need," said Stanley as he still felt the buzz of his first performance.

William laughed at Stanley's simile and wondered if a lightning strike made his hair stick up in the air.

The scene paused as both Jesus and Donald entered the room and stood near to where both young performers sat.

"This is an excellent example of where particle interaction takes effect, Donald," said Jesus as he looked towards both comedians.

Donald looked confused. "I must have missed something, I'm sorry I don't quite understand," was his response though tried hard not offend Jesus.

"All particle interaction laws never stem from the similar course or create comparable outcomes. This event is unusual, but it did happen, and this example could happen to anyone at any time. Let me explain," Jesus continued. "This young comedian," he pointed at Stanley Jefferson. "Will become better-known as comedian Stan Laurel, of Laurel and Hardy fame, and the rest they say is history." Donald showed a look of surprise; he just heard a part of Glasgow history he didn't have any knowledge of. Jesus continued, "His love of the theatre would never be enough to take him to the pinnacle of his profession nor would it give him a good enough salary to work in the environment he professed to adore. He may not have had any other chances whatsoever even to be fuelled by a further ambition to work or perform on any stage anywhere. If it was not for one single moment."

"His jokes?" was the apparent response from Donald.

"No, not his jokes, not being here on this particular night or any other associated part of his life up to present. It was only one small part that would set in motion a chain of events that would take young Stanley to the top of his profession, where he would remain for the rest of his life. All events from this day forwards, he would use for future reference," Jesus continued. "The single moment that changed the whole adventure for Stanley was a luckily thrown tomato." Donald looked further confused. "It arrived at a time when he struggled to complete his act, a time when a mere thought flashed into his head, told him to walk off stage and give up any hope of longevity in this precarious occupation and he was close to doing this, very close to giving up a career in the theatre. The role of events that happened on stage, at that time, opened a door for his future career. A single tomato, thrown by someone from the audience, purely at random, struck his hat, then knocked it off his head. One moment in time, in turn, made it roll a few feet in front of him and gave him a spark of an idea. The audience, he noticed, had laughed at his misfortune, so why not continue in the same vein. Let the crowd continue to laugh at his mishap. It was now that he made a move to pick up his hat, trip ever slightly, launch his foot towards the hat, and initiate a rugby-style kick that would propel the floppy headpiece over the limelight's and into the orchestra pit below. By this event, he had changed the direction of his life, by using this example of initiating 'particle interaction'.

"Of course, he didn't know this, but this is how a small part can recreate a more substantial portion of the development of a person's life, which can change a direction in a lifetime. When you walk along a single road and come to a fork junction, you must decide which route to take. Both streets carry different outcomes. You must remember the cheers of an encore for young Stanley?"

As Jesus finished his words, the scene returned to life, and Donald and Jesus again became watchers of the action.

Two well-dressed men appeared at the open door of the dressing room and knocked three times to gain the attention of the two young amateur comedians who both drank beer and smoked cheap cigarettes. One colossal man stood next to a very slight, small figure. Their dress code offered the same look. Both wore black three-piece suits, highly polished black patent shoes adorned their feet, crisp white shirts had a short black tie as a partner, and each had a gold fob chain, which held a watch that lay hidden in their waistcoat pockets. Two bowler hats were removed simultaneously which showed stiff, short hairstyles covered with liquid paraffin or a similar hair product that set their hair into solid matter.

The large gent had a small toothbrush moustache perched below his nose, spoke, "Sniffer and Sniffer at your service, gentleman." The bowler hats were replaced, and the smaller man produced a business card which he handed to Stanley. The large man spoke again, "I'm Gilbert Sniffer, and this is my brother, Harold. We are Sniffer and Sniffer theatrical agents extraordinaire."

Both spoke simultaneously, "We have a nose for talent," and they giggled. Young Stanley was impressed. He thought this would be the way forwards. Get an agent, get more work and get a break into show business. Become a professional act. "I've never thought about an agent. Tonight was my first ever performance. Could you help me get work?" Stanley said with a quiet, yet hopeful voice.

"Not just work, kind fellow!" the fatter brother growled. "*À cheval donné on ne regarde pas less dents*." Vocals blasted out at pace from the mouth of Gilbert Sniffer in a confident yet pompous manner and in one smooth hand motion produced a napkin from his top pocket, as if a magician waved the perfumed cloth below his nose in a hope to alleviate some of the stomach-turning smells.

"Exactly," said his slim brother, Harold, with a gentle, yet pleasant voice.

"I don't know what that means," said Stanley.

"Nor do I," added William.

"Okay, in a more reluctant form of explanation, I rush to riposte and will revert the simple sentence to the Queen's English for this occasion, only. What I said was, don't look a gift horse in the mouth," Gilbert provided in a confident, yet arrogant way.

"Exactly," repeated Harold.

"Ah," said the 15-year-old Stanley Jefferson, though he gave a stupefied look on his thin, gaunt face, he scratched his head as if he gave serious thought to a question. Whimsically, his fingers rubbed his scalp, which made his hair stick upwards and his lips pouted, he provided a face that looked as though it didn't quite grasp the sense of the question. A puzzled look of a simpleton was the desired effect, and it worked. William's eyes opened wide and his eyebrows raised high into his brow, and he laughed at the actions of Stanley as he continued to play the clown to his small audience. Luckily, Stanley noticed the reaction William gave to his portrayal of an ignoramus. *He would use this move again,* he thought.

"We have a national list of contacts that we could use to promote and develop your name. Just imagine this. Stanley Jefferson, the funniest man in the world. The song and dance man with a comedic genius with a seriously clever wit." He raised his arms to action his words. "I can see your name lit outside theatres all over the country. Stanley Jefferson…"

Stanley interrupted him before he continued his further ambitions, "I don't want to sing or dance. I want to be paid to make people laugh."

The moment froze again.

"This is not just about Stanley's road to success or his future achievements that you witnessed here tonight. It's also about the young friend that sits next to him," added Jesus and he continued,

"A young comedian with similar ambitions, the same dreams and aspirations. With a genuine hope to follow in the footsteps of his heroes, some he had watched from the stalls. He had laughed at many funny dance routines, silly antics and heard stupid jokes. He possibly read about them in newspapers, saw promotional posters around town where their happy smiley faces appeared blatant among the headlines and jump out from the page at him. Having heard a loud blaring voice of a newspaper hawker promote names of theatre stars in the hope of a sale and some occasions, if lucky, meet the stars as they were leaving the stage." He continued as Donald stared at the people in the frozen scene that lay before him,

"This juncture was a defining moment in the life of both young men. All the particles that collided with them at this point developed and shaped their future existence. Whether it was young Stanley sparked a career that would generate millions of fans around the world and leave behind a long legacy of fame that would endure forever on film." Jesus walked around the room slowly but told the story.

"On the other hand, young William here (he said as he pointed an outstretched arm towards him) went on another route of discovery. His future did not follow that of Stanley, not in the least. He did his duty and followed friends to recruit for the Great War eight years from this point. Aged-27, he joined the Highland Light Infantry, the Battalion where most of his pals enlisted. Those men gave up so much to fight another forsaken war. To be led towards death. Volunteers walk blindly into conflict to disillusionment and, eventually, radicalisation of the ranks. Each soldier becomes a small cog in a giant killing machine. They grew hatred in their hearts. Only a small foothold of respect for relatives back home would remain stuck in their desperate hopes and wishes for any human normality which remained in them. It was only with this little grasp of reality, they could keep within their ever-darkened soul, a time that was no longer a route they chose." Jesus finished his words and turned to look at the expression Donald had on his face.

The room and its participants came to life once again; the lingered odour was still awful, the gas lights still emitted a dark, putrid smoke filled the room which had discoloured the walls and left a tar-like residue layer on most fixtures. The further mix of cigarette smoke, gas oil, sweat and a general lack of proper sanitation filled the room with an unbearable odour. All artists similarly started their careers in such conditions, and Stanley and William were no different.

Just then, a lovely young woman, possibly in her early twenties, wore a long cream linen embroidered dress that was raised from the floor and approached her ankles which in turn, showed a twin leather pair of shiny Manhattan buttoned boots. Sage green and red cloche hat covered most of her head with some waves of brown, curly hair that fell to the sides of her charming face. She stuck her head into the room while she held the front of the four-panelled door. "That's me ready, Bill," she said, as she looked as though she had rushed to get to the dressing room at this time. She smiled at the two well-dressed agents and offered a comment to Stanley. "Great routine, Stanley, the girls thought you were a minikin. So cute and tremendously funny. Very afternoonafied, Stanley, very afternoonafied indeed!" she smiled and had Stanley blushing at the compliment. Young William jumped from his seat and gave a few fumbled words for excuses as he grabbed his hat from the table and headed for the door. He kissed the young woman on the cheek, said his goodbyes and both left the room.

The scene re-opens outside the stage door as William and his girlfriend leave the theatre. The moment freezes again. It shows William and his girlfriend captured in mid-step, holding hands and looked lovingly at each other, they made their way into a late evening many, many years ago. Their frozen appearance made them look like two marble figurines installed at the entrance to an impressive Roman temple from ancient times. Possibly presented an allegorical realism, of time where beauty is forever eternal, and dreams come true.

Jesus speaks, "This young man, William, and his partner, Morganna Stone, met over a year ago in another Glasgow theatre where she was a member of a troupe of trained acrobats and dancers that had travelled from New York City many months previously. The dancers had appeared with much success all over the British Isles, built up such a reputation that they were demand in all the top venues in Europe, let alone Britain or Broadway. And, on the final dates of the grand tour, which was here in Glasgow, she met and fell in love with this amiable young man. He, at that time, was a junior stagehand. Working, employed many for many hours as the head of the theatre property department. Erecting and dismantling stage props, repair and build new ones. Paint and decorate scenes or backdrops. Also working with a multitude of materials that were kept in stock – chairs and stools, flags and poles, boxes and baskets, hats and helmets, crowns and jewels, period costumes from different eras, and weaponry and armour all needed for the many variety performances that appeared in the theatre.

"But William's best asset was the fact that his reliability was celebrated by his employers and he would work all given hours to earn more money to assist his parents and siblings. All 13 of them shared a single-end tenement. He ran errands for the performers to make a few extra coins. Promoted a local Gin-shop so the theatre stars could have a place to unwind after a strenuous evening's work, an environment where they could sit and relax in peace and comfort with other performers, and well away from the snooping eyes of the public, or more importantly, the press! All of which earned him more income. Though he always yearned for one chance to appear on stage."

He continued,

"Morganna was born and raised in Cooperstown, New York, to Mary and Jack Stone. Although the youngest of ten children, Morgana was destined to enter the world of music and dance, and by the age of 16, and much to the annoyance and extreme anxiety of her parents, she left to join a dance group based in central New York City. A dance group that used unicycles, pogo sticks, skipping ropes and roller skates in their act, added to the extremities of skills required for the most excellent stage performers of that generation and she mastered all of them. Although trained in ballet, Morganna could apply her talent to mostly any mental or energetic performance which highlighted the quality she had, and, in turn, added to the standard of production required from their ensemble. The troupe was initially set up in 1900 and was formerly known as The Foxton Fury, a Vaudeville promoter with the same name, Foxton Fury, created this group which he hand-picked himself. To build and develop a portfolio of speciality acts within the genre of showbiz. A collective of talent as he continually advertised.

"In a brief period, other talent spotters required the services of the Foxton Furies. The girls had worked solidly without a single day's holiday for nearly two years from January 1900. Top shows like Chris and the beautiful lamp, and Aunt Hanna. All gave a real professional appeal to the girl's hard-work standards that made them a very well sought-after act. On Broadway especially. However, an offer to send the 'Foxton Furies' over the pond to the UK for a substantial amount of money was an offer Fury could not refuse. A London impresario sent a telegraph request to him, saying he sought a skilful troupe of dancing girl performers, to appear on the same bill as many of Britain's famous and rising stars in the infamous Music Hall circuit, which would start on August 1903. This job would last a year or so, and the girls were all in agreement that this chance to work overseas may be a springboard they needed to catapult them to a higher level – a significant opportunity to get a start in the rumoured new lucrative business of moving pictures being mentioned over in California. Reports stated that there was so much work for all sorts of performers, it became the new gold rush.

"To a group of young women, this was an adventure of sorts. The group, now known as the Foxettes, left New York on Tuesday the 4th October 1904 on the Ocean Liner RMS Carpathia, one of The White Star fleet of ships which landed between four to five days later at Liverpool. Famously remembered as the first ship to arrive at the sinking of the Titanic in 1912 and take some 705 souls safely to New York. Also, on board, on the trip to Liverpool, though he had no connection with Morganna or her friends, was the prominent and foremost theatre architect of his generation, Thomas White Lamb, who, many years later, designed such notable venues such as Maddison Square Gardens and The Ziegfeld Theatre on Broadway." Jesus made the scene active once again, and the young couple came back to life and moved forwards laughed and giggled as they left the building. They smartly walked from the New Wynd Lane onto the main thoroughfare Trongate.

Jesus pronounced, "Let's fly, Donald." And soon, they soared high above the city, floated among the cauliflower-shaped cumulus clouds and the top of these clouds showed bright white clumps when lit by the sun. It was a beautiful vision below, Donald's face beamed with glory and he smiled with sheer contentment as he moved freely through the air in the serenity of peace and freedom.

Glasgow Cathedral

It was late afternoon. The sky suddenly darkened, and a cold wind had advanced over Glasgow and brought with it a flurry of powdered snow which dusted the streets and buildings comparable to icing sugar sprinkled over a Victoria sponge cake. Donald's eyes refocused as he looked around the space he found himself. The light was poor, though he gathered a thought that the orange glow of illumination that skimmed the lower walls and flooded floors was that of interior security lights of some sort. He realised he sat on a church pew in a building he recognised well. Beside him sat Jesus. Donald was aware he was in the 12th century gothic Glasgow Cathedral as many of his childhood days spent on regular visits to the beautiful yet mysterious old edifice with his mother and, occasionally, his grandparents. The church sat proudly on Castle Street, had no visitors at this time and looked as if it was closed to the public.

"You must have many questions you want to ask me?" said Jesus with a trusting voice. Donald had many issues his mind told him. "What do you want to ask me?" offered Jesus.

Donald nodded his head slightly and compressed his lips till he succeeded to find a suitable question, "Well, all I can ask is why me? Why did you come to meet with me for something I said when I was a boy?" Donald laid out his first request in a private, yet shy manner.

"It's not what you said as a boy, Donald. It's more about many changes you have made to the lives of others. That's why I'm here." Jesus stood and faced Donald.

Donald looked puzzled. He still didn't understand any of this strangeness. None of this experience made any sense.

Just then, Jesus stood and spoke,

"You have changed the lives of several people. Importantly, you gave hope, shared a vision of peace and offered love to those, where your life crossed over theirs." Jesus faced Donald. "An American author once wrote; 'Kindness is a language which the deaf can hear and the blind can see.'

"So, you see, there is no perfect choice to make in life, not for anyone. It is how the individual decides which road to walk and the choices made on that journey, that can make or break future ambitions of any given life. Create a simple decision, however small it may be, and this can change the route of life for this individual forever. It may also alter the direction of an individual's future, and the path for their family over generations to follow. With your actions, Donald, you caused vibrations to reverberate through the lives of three people that in turn harmonised with reproductions of many more souls. More than you would ever imagine."

Jesus offered his hand to Donald which he accepted. Jesus continued,

"Do you remember this moment?"

The Clyde

The river, Clyde, Thursday 2.15 am, December 17th, 1987.

In a flash, they both stood as viewers on a dark, cold night from a time long past. On a bridge that Donald had crossed many times. Donald looked with eager eyes towards a young man stood close to the edge, above one of the segmental sandstone arches that support the bridge he knew as the Victoria Bridge, which sat solidly above the River Clyde. They both walked a few feet forwards to view the situation that was unfurled before them. A man in his twenties held the outside edge of the granite parapet balusters and had his feet precariously lodged onto a stonework edge of just a few inches in width. A strong wind gained force, which brought severe weather conditions. Two men were in conversation. Jesus and Donald were invisible to both, they approached and listened to the discussion. Jesus spoke, "December, 1987. You were 21 years old." They both listened to the conversation.

"All I would say is, just think about your family and friends," said the young man on the bridge as he nervously reacted to the man who is prepared to jump to his death.

He spoke again, "Life isn't that bad. There must be someone you care for, someone that loves you?", Donald was eager to talk at length to a man with a desperate mind, held in an extreme position and someone that looked drained of passion.

"Maybe the best is yet to come!" Donald said with a sincere voice.

The sad man spoke without turning his head, as the young man hoped to persuade him otherwise, stood his distance.

He tried hard to force an outcome he wished and prayed for, to humanly provide influence on the jumper. He held both hands palm down at chest height, and pumped the air a few inches at a time, in a way that he hoped would stop the man from doing something silly. Like jump!

"I have no one, and no one cares about me. I'm a mess! My life is going nowhere," he said in a deep and sorrowful shaken voice. He thought the young man had stepped closer to him. "Don't move or I'll jump. Get back!" he said loud and to the point. He turned to face the young man and could see he still stood a few feet from him and hadn't moved. The conversation made him relax a little.

The young man spoke loud and clear, and stated his intentions. "I'm not! I promise. Please talk to me. I'm willing to listen to whatever you need to say. Please!" His hands were doing the repeated palm down motion again.

The sad man turned back to look down at the water.

"Look, if you jump, I will come in after you. I promise you that," said the young man with a deliberate and forceful voice.

The sad man paused and didn't speak. He talked, but the young man didn't hear his words.

"I don't want to get wet. It looks cold and murky," added the potential life saver. "We could go for a coffee or a nice meal. Whatever your wish? Just say!"

"I have nothing. I have no future. I lost my job because of my indulgence of alcohol. I have no house, I'm homeless with no money, and all my immediate family have left me. I have no close friends or relatives that I can plead to for help. So, you see, there is no point in living. No one will bat an eye if I jump – a few headlines in a local paper or a mention on the mainstream news. That's it. The end. I don't need any more crap thrown in my face." He rushed the words into one long sentence. He added more words as if he gave a dying man's last testimony, "Two men, last night, urinated on me as I slept outside a shop in Sauchiehall Street. I pleaded with them to leave me alone, but they didn't listen. They laughed. I had nothing to give them; they knew I had nothing to give them.

They just wanted to abuse me for what I had become, not for who I was. They kicked my head. I spat out two teeth, and I also think I may have a broken bone in my leg."

He turned to face the young man on the bridge, which now showed the severity of his facial injuries. Young Donald squirmed at the sight of the man's injuries. His face was bruised and swollen, and possibly stained with dried blood which mixed with his dangly, longish, unkempt, dirty hair and dishevelled unshaved facial growth. Due to severe trauma, his right eye was entirely closed and had developed a sizeable blood-filled hematoma that gave him little or no sight. His other eye was similarly damaged but remained open ever so slightly.

The lonely man also had an enlarged and very swollen bottom lip which must have caused him pain when he talked. He looked dismal, and the young man realised he had a big task ahead of him just to stop the man from suicide. He will try though – he thought. At least, he would keep going to save this life.

The Good Samaritan gave thought to appropriate words, to assist his willingness to provide a solution, his pause in thought allowed the jumper to speak again. *Maybe this is the perfect solution,* thought the do-gooder. *Let him chatter away all night!*

"I saved a crow once," was the few words he spoke but not words the lifesaver had expected.

"You saved a crow?" he hoped he could allow the jumper time to elaborate his story which in turn would keep him from the pitch-black, icy Clyde. It worked, and the sad fellow continued with his story.

"When I was a young boy, I was at a school camp, a summer retreat, an educational holiday of sorts. I was with a few pals, and we played 'hide and seek' in nearby woods, close to the wooden huts where we slept. When I tried to find the right place to hide among the birch and bracken, I discovered a young crow caught in a trap – a wooden box covered with wire mesh or some chicken wire. It was a prison for the bird. The bird was frantic and very much distressed. It flapped its wings constantly, gave a horrible scream noise that made me cringe. There were a few other crows close by, but they couldn't help with this situation, they just watched. I was afraid of the crow as much as I feared the terrible trap that imprisoned it. I looked for any way possible where I could let the bird escape from this hell it found itself. I turned the cage over repeatedly, looked for a hatch or some open space in the cage to give the bird freedom. The bird was fearful. It didn't scream anymore, but it fluttered its wings more and more, in a very distressing way. Then, luckily, I noticed a small flap that was locked in place with a clip of sorts.

"I grasped this, and pulled and pushed with all my strength till the flap gave way, and thankfully, opened a small space to the outside world. It was now I had to entice the little bird to freedom. It jumped and flapped against every side of the enclosed cage until it managed to sense the way to freedom from this suppression it was in, was through the small space I had found. It did. It flew from the cage to join other crows that had watched the scenario unfurl before them. Then, in a moment, the group took flight and disappeared far and deeper into the woods. I felt good. I thought that I had done something remarkable. Something that made me feel proud. Proud that I saved a life. I didn't want to consider what the outcome would have been for the crow if I hadn't wandered by chance to find this cage and it's captive.

"Destroy the prison. Destroy it all, was the thought that came to mind. I stamped my right foot in anger, repeatedly, over the fragile frame that was robust enough to hold a small, scared bird, but not my right foot as I kept on stamping, then jumped on the cage. I destroyed the bird jail.

"It would capture no more birds. It was, as I later discovered, a trap to catch crows or magpies who the local estate owner thought they ate the eggs of the landowner's pheasant stock. I never believed that story then, and I don't buy it now."

He continued, "I had finished my necessary action, and I felt satisfied. My bare legs suffered most in this deed. My uncovered shins showed a few patches of loose skin. There were many scratches and bruises with trickles of blood ran down my legs towards my socks, the wire mesh had taken spiteful revenge on me, I'm sure. I was a hero without a medal. After I saved the bird's life, I felt good. I did something right." He paused again. Looked down towards the Clyde. He continued, "It was after this event, a surreal period of my life began." He paused again.

The young Samaritan could hear a voice in his head talk to him. It was a loud clear and purposeful voice. The voice repeated: *Go on, Johnny-on-the-spot, save this poor man's life. He needs you!* Donald's look was perplexed and disturbing; his action was to shake his head several times with a hope to relieve this gruff voice from his mind. He wanted to edge forwards but decided against any sudden movement. The depressed figure looked weary as both Jesus and Donald listened to the continuing story. "Unbelievably, one of the strangest things ever to happen to me, happened shortly on my return home from summer camp." The cold night air was now beginning to seep into both men, but the sad homeless man was near collapse. His face had turned bluish, his hands looked numb as the air bit into every part of his scantily dressed frame, and he swayed slowly as if near fainting. The weather remained poor, and the wind-chill factor made both men bitterly cold and miserable. The conditions continued to worsen, and together, they began to realise that this moment could not last much longer. Though the lifesaver was more than happy to hear more of the sad man's story, the jumper continued,

"About a week or so after I returned home, I began to feel poorly. I had contracted the measles virus. I lay in bed for nearly a month with the usual impediment of a runny nose, persistent coughing and watery, inflamed eyes. A few days later, a red, flat rash appeared on my face, then soon it covered my entire body and consolidated me with an irritating and severely itchy skin, which I could not stop scratching. It was then, as my mother would say, I hit a high fever. I was insane at times. I was unwell and got worse. In my case, further complications set in and I contracted viral pneumonia, which the pleasurable doctor prescribed with a shortlist of complete rest, plenty of liquids and a course of antibiotics. In addition to a batch of vitamin A tablets, I had to swallow with a sip of warm water or a gulp of Ferguzade. All of which kept me bedridden. I was quarantined and slept alone. After school hours, I could hear my friends at play in the local park near to my house. Laughing, joking, kicked a ball and there was me: lying ill in bed and feeling sorry for myself.

"It happened then.

"I was lying on my back with two raised pillows, puffed-up and wedged behind my head. My mum said this was to build my energy, for reasons only known to her.

"At first, I thought it was my mum or my brother playing a game with me. A soft, irregular tapping noise that emanated from somewhere in my bedroom. Tap, tap, tap. The sound was relentless. Tap, tap, tap.

"I was weak and sore, had little strength to move, or leave the warmth of my bed to search for the din that still participated; to my annoyance. I turned on my side and covered my head with the candlewick bedspread to avoid hearing the recurrent sound. It did stop, and after a few minutes, I pulled the covers back from my face and grabbed the first comic I could lay my hands on."

Young Johnny-on-the-spot wilted under the severe weather. He couldn't understand why the man on the ledge could muster a story at this time. Donald knew that all hope flowed fast from both men. He listened but didn't want to be there. He thought of home and a warm bed. But the voice repeated, even more evident this time, *If anyone can save this man's life, it's you, Johnny-on-the-spot. Go on, keep him safe, give him hope!*

The suicidal man was talking; he gave his last statement in his miserable life.

"Commando, do you know this comic?" he continued and heard no response. "I was engrossed in the war stories of Commando. All storylines based on symbolic motifs. You know? The usual stuff, cowardice, bravery, King and country, heroic actions, made a brew of tea while in the face of danger. A comic that draws themes from both world wars."

The young lifesaver smiled at his recollection of this comic which he read also.

"Then the tapping started again," the homeless man said. "But I knew where it came from now. I used whatever strength I could muster to pull myself upwards and out of bed. I slowly took a few steps to prepare my balance and walked a further few short steps towards the window. I gently held the edge of one side of the curtain to open it more to allow more light to enter the room. And there it was." He paused again.

"One of your friends?" said the do-gooder in response.

"No, not a friend. Not then. Not at that time. But it became a very close and dear friend in the years to come." The young man could not offer another question. He waited for more information from the man on the ledge.

"It was a crow," he said quietly.

"A crow?" responded young Donald.

"Yes, a real crow. I managed to open the window, and it came inside. It just stood on the sill and stared at me. I fed him uneaten fruit that overflowed from a bowl that sat on a bedside table which he devoured favourably."

"Do you believe the bird you saved at school camp is the same bird that visited you at home?" asked the younger man curiously.

"Yes. It was the same bird. It is the only real friend I have had my entire life," he exclaimed.

Now, being prepared for two outcomes, the do-gooder took a step forwards, and towards the man on the edge of the bridge. "Please hold my hand. We can at least talk in a more comfortable place."

He froze in his tracks, possibly realised that another step may make the man jump.

The man on the ledge slowly turned to face the lifesaver. He held the parapet insecurely, slightly lost his footing, though he managed to regain a secure balance of sorts. A look of contentment flowed over his face as his feet shuffled again, still unsteadily on the small sandstone ledge.

"I assume you are Donald Forbes?" the man on the ledge asked.

"Of course, my name is Donald Forbes. How on Gods earth would you know that?"

Move and grab the poor wretch, Donald thought. *Maybe get a solid grip on his hand then lead him to the safety of the walkway. Or better still, dive towards him and seize hold of his arm. Or catch any part of him.*

"Well, Donald Forbes, I am Jonathon Dailly, and it was a pleasure to have met you. Even though it is far too late.

"Thank you, thank you for the offer of help, and showing kindness to me. Just remember this, Donald. Your life is now as it will always be!"

And, in an instant, he took a step backwards, plummeted down towards to icy cold dark and murky waters of the Clyde. In the stillness that surrounded him, he heard an enormous splash as the weak body hit the water. While the rain, and bitterly cold wind enveloped the young body of Donald Forbes.

Young Donald was shocked by this event. His body stopped moving for a second before he could react or make any judgement, to the blood-curdled noise of the body contacting the water. The splash and the impact reverberated through young Donald Forbes by bearing witness to such a tragic event. He moved fast now, he looked over the bridge edge to look for a sign of the man in the water. It was too dark to see the surface and the harsh, bitter inclement weather added to his wrath of any attempted rescue. Could he do this, he asked himself.

He raised his head from the edge then looked to the opposite side of the bridge to where he ran. Donald checked for traffic, but the place was quiet and saw no other person except a vehicle approaching from the city centre. He ran over the snow-covered bridge, leapt towards the ice-shielded parapet, sat precariously upon it, froze for a second and looked back over the bridge to see that the vehicle on approach was a police Ford Granada MK11 which approached from Stockwell Street. Donald lost interest in the police car, and his attention turned to hear the man in the water struggle, just below his view. He promptly removed his long black overcoat, which he thought would hamper his rescue, even though it was a freezing night, he threw it to the ground. Took another glance at the police car, then jumped.

The police officers in the squad car had witnessed the man jump and had reacted skilfully. The driver applied a spin that moved the vehicle over to the west side of the bridge where the young man had dropped, the blue light emergency beacon flashed repeatedly and red flashing hazard lights operated as a self-promotional awareness to any vehicle that passed. "We are here, we are in control, and we are in command of this situation. Back off!"

The officer in charge was fast to instigate the circumstance by given instructions to the young constable; check and locate the jumper, retrieve the jumper. He leapt from the car even though it hadn't entirely stopped, the young constable slipped on the slippery underfoot surface but managed to stay upright. His first response was to check the river from the closest vantage point from where the man had leapt and hoped to see or hear noise from below.

The senior police officer, on the other hand, picked up the twisted chord held radio transmitter and pressed the large black button that protruded from the side of the microphone. "Alpha 2 to control, Alpha 2 to control, urgent 21, there is a person in the Clyde. Victoria bridge at Clyde Street over. Request EMS in assistance, over." He didn't wait or listen to the control room response as he was out of the squad car in seconds and speedily moved to the rear of the vehicle. His young colleague now ran from the bridge towards Clyde Street, which had a riverside walkway that sat lower than the old arched-framed Victoria conduit, that had more reachable access to the river. As he clutched a safety line, which the senior officer had acquired from the boot of the vehicle, he ran towards the area where the young constable stood. The rope was thrown into the dark water repeatedly, in the hope that someone may reach for the lifeline. The night was cold and dark with visibility poor and rescue, he knew, would be a small possibility. However, the officers guessed by the faint noises heard on the river, emanating in from the darkness of the Clyde, that someone was close to the river edge and spent further time using the rope and hoped the jumper may take hold of this lifeline.

Both Jesus and Donald remained viewers of the scene. They now stood close to the police officers, watching them desperately attempt a rescue. A rescue by any means and by any means possible. If not saving of life, then a body, or possibly two, would be found dead in the icy water at some point.

Young Donald was desperate. He clung to a fellow human being, a person he never knew. Filled with lactic acid, his muscles tired by the continual tensioned grip he held around the victim's chest, he began to lose his weak grasp. But now the cold started to cause serious trouble for both men. They were pulled down fast by the undercurrent and bobbed up several times in succession. Donald lost body heat and became disorientated, and hypothermia began to take hold. Sucked into the cold depths of the river as they struggled to stay afloat. Again, they bobbed up, for a heavenly offer of fresh air; cold, bitter fresh air that stabbed his throat and lungs as it passed through his blue lips that accepted the gift of oxygen. Any oxygen was welcomed.

His head was stirred with the flow of cold air that entered his body, he tried in earnest to suck as much in as possible, in a vain attempt to pump much-needed blood through his body which he hoped would rush to surround his vital organs and keep them fed with much-needed nutrients.

He continually tugged and pulled with all his might on the helpless soul, but some object or debris was not ready to let its catch go smoothly. The river kept wrapping its cold fingers around both men and held them forcefully in the grasp of death.

This man chose death by drowning.
And sink into the icy water he will.
The river was now in charge.

Young Donald was being dragged more in-depth into the icy cold extremities of the dark waters by the high tide which drew and swayed both men as if bobbing apples in a bathtub. As Donald bounced weakly under the water, a bright light filled the area before him, his eyes only just bore witness to the effect, a view which he thought was the end of his life. A route to heaven. A place where warmth would await him. Follow the light. He was slipping away, and his suicidal friend would take him along the early road to the afterlife.

"Come on, Johnny-on-the-spot, go towards the light. The light will help you. Wake up, Johnny-on-the-spot. Wake up!" were the last words he heard before he slipped into an unconscious state, as his previous conscious breath left his dying body. His head slumped backwards, and his body flopped lifelessly in the water as he began to float downstream.

At the rescue scene, on the river's edge, the police officers had been joined by an ambulance and a local fire engine crew. Hopefully, very soon, a small motorboat from the Glasgow Humane Society would arrive to aid the rescue.

On its way, from a short distance from its base on the Glasgow Green, the river man, the sole lifeguard in the approaching motor boat, propelled the craft through the Clyde tidal weir. The rough weather, moreover, created a perilous journey ahead and would make any rescue desperate. He also knew too well, after years of experience working on the River Clyde, that when the tide and weather operated together, this would make any rescue difficult. Moving at the best speed possible, the boat raced forwards.

The emergency services personnel worked hard to assist the man in the water, who was now visible under the lights of several torches, to give a rescue every chance of success, however slight it was.

Just then, and out with every rule in the book and away from the discipline of his formidable training, the young policeman jumped into the icy water with no consent or agreement from his senior officer. There was no need to complain or shout obscenities or react negatively to the young officer. Not at this time! He had to be professional at this moment, he must continue to save the life of the man. Or save both men now. The emergency crews acted in the manner of an experienced and accomplished group of professionals, and organised themselves in a well-drilled exercise that years of quality training brought. He would berate the young officer later. He will read the riot act to him. That's if he can get him out of the water.

A powerful Francis searchlight mounted high on the fire engine now shone on the river which significantly floodlit the area where the man struggled to stay afloat. The ground services watched keenly as the young police officer had approached the man and made good, a solid grip around his chest just below his arms, which was the technique he had gained at a well-qualified rescue drill during his cadet years at the Police College at Tulliallan in Fife, though he thought would never require such a procedure. The small motorboat had now arrived at the scene and stopped close by both men. The engine still hummed to limited sound as the power reduced to a low level, so that it ticked over and ready to move off at pace when required.

The weather conditions remained severe which added to the struggle of a natural rescue. Both men in the water were static in one position as the boat glided slowly to stop near them or as close as the conditions served. Instantly, the river man made a move towards the water, and took hold of the young constable at his collar and pulled with all his might, managed to tear off an emblem from one side of his police jacket which he disregarded into the river. He continued to assist both men by pulling them towards the boat. Shouting to the young officer and told him to climb aboard the vessel which would give him added support to help the man moored to the debris of the Clyde, to hopefully free him from his anchorage.

Doing all possible actions to support this struggle, he gave an assured appraisal of the situation to the officer and explained his knowledgeable rescue plans.

Using all the strength he could muster, he managed to wrench the officer onto his boat while keeping the other man close. A rope held the man in the water tightly, by a knot which was protected securely by a Midshipman's hitch that had been tied firmly to a pad eye on the boat hull. Both men worked frantically to pull the man to liberty, they tugged and heaved until the river eventually released its catch which in turn caused a massive splash of water that engulfed the small craft, with cold, dirty water. The boat now spun uncontrollably in the water as both lost their footing, it made them fall head first towards the bow of the boat. A powerful scream left the mouth of the young officer as his head took the brunt of the fall which split his scalp in the centre of his skull and caused a deep gash where excessive blood spurted from it. He was conscious but stunned and in need of immediate medical attention. The river man had fallen to the side of the boat but never lost hold of the rope that held the poor man in the water, in a position close to his craft. He knew by the fall he had damaged or possibly broken a rib just by the extreme pain. He felt sick, and he expulsed several mouthfuls of vomit. *The pain was not a fundamental problem at this time,* he thought. He needed to get both men to shelter and safety on the shoreline that gave him the strength of thought.

The Clyde released its captives from its solid grip, now he must be saved from the water. A good hold of the lifeless victim, the river man, with practical experience of using his well-used technique, used on many occasions over many years, crouched on his knees, lifted the man up and over the side of the craft, and lay him gently on the floor of his boat. His actions gave him much pain, but he did what he set out to do, and that was to save a life. All this work was viewed from the riverbank much to the delight of emergency staff that had watched this successful liberation. A few cries of congratulations and several hand-clap responses filtered through the air towards the lifeboat.

This situation was not near completion. The Glasgow Humane Society man grasped the outboard steering handle with a fiercely tight grip, in readiness to move at full throttle. He shouted aloud, hoping that the emergency services on terra firma could hear his orders but knew his verbal offerings would be in vain, but the rescuers recognised he would head back towards the GHS pier a few minutes of a rough ride upstream where he would disembark with both patients. The revs on the outboard motor raced at a very high level as the boat span through the tidal river, bounced disorderly on the water and struggled to keep balance, though controllable, with the extra weight it was now carrying. But forwards it went. The small launch disappeared into the darkness of the night as it skipped over the Clyde, away from the torch and light beams. The champion in his boat followed his instinct and the knowledge he had of this enigmatic river, understood the urgency of such an event and did everything in his power to return the two men to the safety of the shore. The boat raised water as it flew from the scene.

Jesus and Donald observed the scene as the emergency services move from the area and made haste to Glasgow Green, where they would once again assemble to achieve a proper and definite conclusion to this event. Donald was quiet, as his gaze faced the cold and bitter Clyde of late 1987.

The weather retained its clutch of the moment as Donald spoke, "I died. I am dead!" He turned and stared at Jesus.

Jesus took his stare and spoke to Donald.

"What do you remember of this night?"

"I remember jumping from the bridge. That's all I can recollect," Donald said.

"Is that all?"

Donald looked back towards the river.

"My mind is blank," he paused before turned again to look at Jesus.

"I am dead. I can't recollect one thing. Not one thing after I jumped from the bridge. I drowned, I drowned," he spoke fearfully and continued.

"Am I dead?" he looked for an answer. He looked dismayed.

The police car came to a sudden stop. It arrived alongside the ambulance that had parked close to the Glasgow Human society building situated on the north side of Clyde, on the Glasgow Green. Two medics ran towards the berthed lifeboat on the GHS pier and assisted the repatriation of the liberated souls. The first man showed no signs of life, and the paramedics swiftly laid him on the ground and proceeded to give five first rescues breaths. Then CPR as they applied chest compressions, then two more rescue breaths until the casualty spat an excess of dirty Clyde water from his mouth. The paramedics sighed with relief on a job well done but acted fast by carrying the man to the warmer environment of the ambulance – where one medic covered him with blankets and strapped him securely to the stretcher bed while checking his breathing, his pulse and a level of response by continually asking his name. Assisting the young police officer was now on the agenda, and soon, he, too, was in the comfort of the ambulance. He showed few signs of severe trauma, but a deep laceration on his head was cleaned with a sterilised veil which stopped the bleeding for the time being. A padded bandage covered the wound as a precaution, though a few stitches and a subsequent headache would likely follow suit.

The young officer was cold and looked in a bewildered state as the sergeant walked towards the ambulance to view the situation and see how his young colleague fared.

The senior officer stood near the ambulance rear doors as if an army major inspecting his troops on a parade ground. The young officer viewed his sergeant as he stood, surveying the mess he found himself in, he felt sick and tired. The sergeant leant forwards and tapped the young constable's shoulder and spoke in a soft (and unusual for him), voice, "Good job, lad, bloody good job." The young officer managed a faint glimmer of a smile and felt an immense sense of pride flow through him that aided his recovery somewhat, well, he thought so. Yet, he was sure the aftermath would not be so easy. A total rollicking would not pass him by.

The Glasgow Humane society man stood by his motor launch and held his chest. In deep pain and in need of medical assistance. Sergeant Burke walked towards him.

"Freddie, how are you?" A few facial smirks and groans offered the fact that he could not hide the severity of his injuries, but his reactions tried hard to do so.

"I'm okay, Tom," was his response to an officer he knew.

The ambulance averted their conversation as it drove at speed with flashing lights and a siren boomed loud as it raced towards the Royal Infirmary at the top end of High Street in the Townhead area.

Both men turned to watch the vehicle disappear.

"I am fine, Tom, it's only a few bruises. My pride has been dented," offered the lifeguard, though he still showed signs of discomfort.

"How long have I known you, Freddie? A few years now, I'm guessing. And long enough to understand you are not entirely honest with me. Remember, I've tasted the tea you make, and that's not the best cuppa in Glasgow as you always remind me, now is it?" said the sergeant as he took Freddie's arm.

"Let's get you to hospital, Freddy," he said walking him to the police car before joining his young colleague at the Royal Infirmary.

As the police car headed off towards the hospital, Freddy offered a comment, "What's wrong with my tea then?"

The ambulance, with both casualties, sped through the snow and storm as it approached the Royal Infirmary. The siren still blared, and the lights flashed which caught the attention of a few late-night revellers and vehicle drivers alike. The stranger strapped to the stretcher bed awoke from a drowsy state.

He looked into the eyes of the paramedic and asked, "How is Donald Forbes? Is he OK?"

Young Constable Shaw and the paramedic heard the stranger repeat the sentence before he fell unconsciousness.

"Donald Forbes? Who is Donald Forbes?" responded Constable Shaw.

The Clydeside

Donald stood with Jesus and stared out over the cold River Clyde, mesmerised by the circumstances of the moments he had borne witness. Sadness enveloped him, depression surged through his body as thoughtful answers he sought seemed so far from his reality – he could not imagine a life – a life where truth would ever again exist, especially after the continual surreal images, his mind suffered, as he had watched the past unravel before him.

"You must remember this moment, Donald," said Jesus, as he broke the silence.

Both suddenly appeared on a rowing boat and stood securely on which seemed a precarious foothold, surrounded by thick snow and hail as the darkness kept its grip now. Laid helpless on the bottom of the vessel was young Donald, apparently rescued from the cold dark river and perched above him, as both oars surged through the water with each motion, was a very young boy.

Ghost-like in appearance. A very grey gaunt young boy with clothes that matched a period of prolonged past. Clothed with a grey shirt, grey woollen V-neck knitted jersey, with grey shorts, grey socks with badly worn black hobnail boots. Both his legs encapsulated in metal callipers that showed signs of polio disease from his earlier life. His demeanour was of joy and his valiant effort made the boat move slowly but surely over the roughening tide of the river, and further disclosed a real determination in his actions. Donald never asked Jesus any more questions, but feelings ran wild through his body, external memories came flooding back. Memories he now remembered, or did he? Something real was happening. His gaze fell on the ghost boy and the boy returned the stare. The ghost boy began to sing, *Row, row, row your boat gently down the stream merrily, merrily, merrily, merrily – life is but a dream.* He said the verse repeatedly as the moment evaporated, as if Donald had fallen into a deep sleep.

Little Boy
December, 1987

It was a cold and brisk sunny morning when young Donald Forbes woke to the sound of a digital clock, a realistic Chronomatic 223 alarm clock to be precise. A loud beep, beep, beep belted out from the radio speaker which would possibly waken everyone in the block, or further afield he imagined, as his hand leant over to press the switch that would render the alarm off with red digital numbers flashing (seven am). As Donald lay still, gathering his morning thoughts, music was heard from another room, in the kitchen, where another small digital radio sat perched on a worktop. The receiver must have been left on last night, he supposed. His apartment, the top flat, a small two-bedroom property that sat in Bathgate Street – on the corner of Reidvale Street in the district of Dennistoun, a suburb of Glasgow, felt chilled and unemotional this early morning, and his first chore would be to put the heaters on and get some warm air circulating.

The red sandstone building stood close to a main arterial railway track which led to Queen Street station in central Glasgow. He used the railway daily for the short trip to the city, where he worked as a barman in a local hotel. Serving 80s classic cocktails such as Harvey Wallbangers, Manhattans and Singapore slings to businesswomen that wore bulky shoulder pads bulging in their oversized blazers, projected big wild hair and showcased bright makeup, while yuppie men wore oversized suits and showed sockless feet in flimsy fabric shoes. And, nigh on everybody in the bar held a Filofax.

"It is just after seven for goodness sake," he spoke taking another glance at the bedside clock to reiterate his first squint at the ticking timepiece.

"Why did I set the bloody alarm?" he said aloud.

He crawled slowly to the bed edge and gave a visual search for any item of clothes he could wear. A pair of faded jeans and a warm Shetland jumper came to hand. He dressed slowly and was unsteady on his feet. His balance was not perfect which made him stumble back to the bed edge, where he pulled on a thick pair of socks and plunged both feet into a well-worn pair of red tanned Doc Martins. Donald ran his hands over his full head of auburn hair which was more of a habit than a custom. Now ready, he glimpsed a look in the small wardrobe mirror, that gave him an impression of a late night spent at some pub or a friend's party, neither which he could recall. His balance returned at this point and managed to head for breakfast. George Michael's new song, *Faith*, played in the background, as the sound of Radio 1 filled the small kitchen. The early morning DJ promoted his show with what he imagined to be, a grinning, ill-bearing smarmy face, with a luvvy attitude. Wore oversized fake medallions strung around his neck loosely and pink coloured sunglasses perched on the edge of his nose, as his high pitch, an over-bearing voice yelled, "Good morning to all listeners out there, have a great day!"

What a prick, he thought.

"What's for breakfast today?" he said to himself as he strolled into the small kitchen that had a table fit for two people and no more. He opened the door of the fridge and pulled out a glass bottle pint of cold milk. Pressed his thumb into the foil cap which released ice-cold moo-juice. A foldable wooden seat was pulled under him. An open box of Rice Crispies filled a clear glass bowl that was more than likely a mixing or ovenproof dish but suited Donald's appetite perfectly. A large spoonful of sugar-covered the cereal which was then swamped with cold milk until a few crispies left the plate and fell onto the plastic table cover which featured a thick strip of black and white zebra print. Donald tucked into his breakfast as if he hadn't eaten for days.

A chrome-plated kettle sat on the table rapidly boiled and exuded vaporised steam through the spout. Grasping the pot handle, Donald promptly poured the liquid into the cup which held instant coffee granules.

But, yet again, he over-stirred the ingredients and had added too much sugar, milk was a forgotten addition that combined with a grimace on his face made him murmur under his breath, "Damn."

The cup was placed on his lips, he drank slowly, he knew heat still lurked in the container. He was relaxed and consumed on breakfast radio's morning show by now. A short slurp of coffee confirmed it was hot and had too much sugar. His leisurely thoughts were soon disturbed by the pitter-patter of footsteps behind him emanating from the hallway, steps gradually advanced towards him and got louder which made him feel so un-at-ease.

He spun around, jumped to his unsteady feet, screamed as if he would collapse with sudden heart failure, dropped the hot coffee which fell onto the linoleum flooring, where the ceramic mug bounced several times before it broke into numerous pieces. The small seat where he sat was kicked back towards the table which in turn tumbled over which made the kettle, the condiments, milk jug and sugar bowl, and leftover breakfast, cover the floor to present a Jackson Pollock type of floor artwork. He froze. Shook violently, he could not speak. A ghost-like character, a figure of a little boy. One he may know!

The small grey translucent figure stood, stared in Donald's direction. He recalled memories now. The little boy in the boat saved his life! The boy in his dream. Recollections flooded to his conscience. It was not a dream, this was real and the small ghost boy saved my life!

Donald stood anchored to the spot. His mind spoke to him.

He felt like a myotonic goat, otherwise known as the fainting goat, where a goat that freezes when shocked, younger goats will stiffen and fall over. He thought he was

101

about to fall over. The adrenalin had slowed his muscles to a sudden stop! He managed to stay upright but swayed gently and rested on a wall near the kitchen doorway.

He could not move, his muscles were rigid as the ghost boy hovered by the entrance to the kitchen. The apparition now held out his right arm which exposed a small sheet of paper. He released it and it fell sluggishly to the floor, and at that moment, the entity disappeared.

Slowly, Donald felt his muscles twitch and contract back to life; movement within his body returned, no longer the myotonic goat. He walked towards the sheet of paper, and swooped slow and low to pick it up. Glanced forwards, he noticed the wooden floor in the hallway covered in water. His observance scanned the hall, floor, ceiling and walls looked for further evidence that the ghost boy was still in the vicinity. The paper was wet and had no visible writing on it. He stared at it, looked on both sides before he placed it on the counter near the sink.

The kitchen needs cleaning, now his mind proclaimed. Returning the table back on its unsteady feet and refolded the wooden chair into a form that looked suitable and supportable. A small brush and dustpan collected most of the mixture of wreckage remains. A recurrent few stares towards the hallway kept him aware of the paranormal activity that had occurred, or may not have? What is going on?

The letter

The small sheet of paper had dried when Donald picked it up. To his disbelief, the article showed words firmly embedded in the once old, wet, blank piece of paper. He stared at the print and began to read the child-like words that flew persuasively into his eyes. His face became pale and sleepy as he drifted into a sleep-like dream. A short film was being projected directly into his mind. As bright as if it was real. He moved towards the small wooden chair and dropped his weight on it. Again, to support his unsteady frame, he placed the note on the table and soon began transporting to another realm of thought. Now he knew he saw something strange, he was being held in a trance by a supernatural force which propelled apparitions of dark illusions, as vivid mental images rushed to fill his immediate thoughts.

He stared one more time at the note before being transported to a confused hallucination, and one that was very real.

Please help me.
My name is Tommy Shaw. I live in 67a Bathgate Street in Glasgow. I want someone to save me. Tommy

Donald was propped up motionless with his back firmly placed against the spindle of the chair. His face stared down towards the table, his chin flopped forwards with his mouth agape, which was held stationary at his chest – his body shook frantically momentarily, then stopped. A clear vision started to penetrate his perception.

Donald's dream illusion:

Three small boys playing, typical boy's games, pushing and hitting each other, laughing and giggling, as they sauntered along a footpath near a river. One boy, the boy Donald saw as the apparition, the boy with a metal calliper on each leg, walked perfectly well (although it would have been extremely trying for the boy after he fell ill to acute polio at a younger age).

Many unfortunate patients live with muscle weakness. That means muscles of arms, trunks and legs could be weaker. Various groups of muscles are involved in multiple patients. Legs are most commonly affected. All of this leads to joint deformities, contracture of tissues which resulted in a limb that is not as functional.

Though with a struggle, he did manage to keep up with his friends, they were a few feet ahead, bouncing wildly as active children do. Young Tommy laughed and clapped hands at the enjoyment of being part of the occasion. As they approached the riverbank, near a crop of small trees and berry bushes which dotted the area, the boys proceeded to play imaginary pirates. Yelled appropriate buccaneer terms and slogans, and viewed the river ahead as a potential escape route from the British Navy. The fun continued, their small round faces looked red with the regular intake of fresh air and active, enjoyable play.

One of the boys, the smallest, a thin, skinny boy with a dirty face, runny nose, and with holes in every item of clothing and black leather clog shoes held in place by brown parcel string, shouted for his friends to join him among the vegetation.

He had found a hidden treasure. He let them both hear this before they reached him. "I have found a pirate's treasure chest!"

The excited boys met amongst the trees and shrubbery where they stared in delight at the new-found prize. "A pirate's chest!" the older of the boy shouted. "Let's move it," he added.

Each grabbed a corner or old handle, two which were bolted at each end of the box, they tugged as they grappled their way through overgrown weeds, jaggy nettles, vines and bushes, skipped over empty beer bottles and disregarded litter – to escape the grip of the mighty jungle.

With an enormous struggle, the boys succeeded in their quest to secure the pirate's sea chest from the grip the tropical forest had on it. They breathed substantial restful sighs of relief but enjoyed the moment of triumph when they eventually managed to tug the heavy box onto a grass clearing close-by the river.

They inspected it thoroughly, the box was spacious enough to accept all three boys inside, was 'a terrific find' as the older boy screamed aloud. It was in a relatively good condition, possibly a worker's toolbox. The rusty red painted container had four faded letters printed on the front side of the box, which clearly stated C S D W.

Donald's mind instantly gave him an explanation of the four-letter code. His vision which was drawn to the letters, which in turn, transformed the letter puzzle into full words for his viewing. The writing appeared clearly visible and stencil-painted white on the strongbox frontage. 'Corporation. Sewage Disposal Works', the words were bright and highly visible. The images in his mind changed again. The lid was wrenched open by the older boy as he raised the worn hasp from the metal looped staple. The box creaked and moaned as the cover flew open and backwards till it was held in position by the three durable hinges. "Empty as my pocket," said the older boy staring interestingly into the void. He patted Tommy on the shoulder.

"Jump into your pirate ship, Tommy. We will sail for home!"

They aided an eager Tommy to enter the chest where he sat and delivered Captain's orders to his crew. He was using an imaginary telescope to tell his pals that another ship approached from the distance. And it had big guns.

"We must prepare for battle. Raise the flag and load the weapons," his little voice bellowed.

"Aye, aye, Captain."

"Get the ship ready to sail, men, we must be ready to fight!"

"The British are sailing towards us fast, Captain. They have more guns than we have."

"Aye, me hearties. Shiver me timbers. Set sail for port and be quick about it."

Young Tommy was Captain and played the role well.

"Why don't we all hide from the British ship and hope she sails by!"

"Good idea," the thin boy said as he winked his right eye towards the older boy.

The two boys forced the lid over and closed it as Tommy complained and screamed for them to stop. The skinny boy leapt his backside on the top of the chest while the older boy closed the hasp over the staple and stuck a solid twig through the loop to lock it firmly. They both hit and kicked the box several times before they ran off. Tommy heard their laughter fade in the distance.

Closed inside the dark box, Tommy could see some limited light shine through a few cracks or holes dotted around metal sides. His cries for help were going unheard, but he could breathe sufficiently. Would someone pass and rescue him? Someone must walk this way. *My friends will return,* he imagined.

Straightaway, a torrential downpour befell the location which made the sobbing boy inside the box stop crying. The falling shower hitting the trunk was amplified many times, and made Tommy feel sad, anxious, scared and alone in the void of inescapable darkness. He wanted to go home.

His mum would be looking for him, and his tea would be ready.

His weak little voice spoke. He spoke to himself. He spoke words of encouragement that his father gave him. His father told him he was better than anyone. His dad said he was a special boy. God created a special boy. God even gave him metal leg braces to make him tough. He was the sturdiest boy in Glasgow, his dad reminded him.

"You are the best of the bunch and don't let anyone tell you differently."

"Go on, Johnny-on-the-spot, get this old rust lid open. Go on, Johnny! You can do it. You are special!" he said repeatedly.

He heaved, and he thrust all the power his small, unfamiliar muscles could deliver – an almighty effort that lasted several minutes. He rocked backwards and forwards till a movement in the box reacted. His eyes lit up. "I can escape. I am a special boy." He shook and rocked more, and the box moved again and again. He shuddered with all his might.

"I am escaping! I will survive!"

The box moved on its own momentum now, and it was soon gaining speed. The entombed little boy screamed as it tumbled over and over on its side, revolved over the sloped ground, crashed over dirt and stones as it flew towards the river. Up and over, around and around, tumbling, tumbling, tumbling. Then, it collided with soft mud, as it made eerie slurping noises as he continued to rock the box repeatedly. Unknown to Tommy, the trunk sat precariously on the riverbank edge. He must escape now! The rusty old casket had stopped moving, and he paused before he would try again, in another vain attempt to force the lid open.

Tommy heard a sound. A strange and horrible clatter. A noise that injected great fear into his tiny body.

It still rained severely. The area where the box previously sat, started to break away from the grip of the central wooded area and slid slowly towards the dark river edge. It was the noise of landfall, a sound that this young life never experienced before, but it made him afraid. The dirt now turned into a viscous liquid. The lack of vegetation at this point of the riverbank, or deep-rooted trees or plants which would typically hold the sediment together – made this riverbank and river wall open to severe erosion. The torrential rain did not help either. The wet earth wall allowed a mighty break where an extreme force brought tonnes of mud sliding down towards the box. This enormous flow of energy made the container tip over and drop downwards, towards the river, where it crashed into more dirt and a deep-lying repugnant slurry at the river's edge.

Tommy screamed until his voice faded. He cried until he could cry no more. So weak and scared. He wanted his mum and dad. He wanted to go home.

Much more dirt and mud toppled down to cover the box completely, then water started to infiltrate the space and entered through holes and cracks around the box. Mud, mud and even more mud enveloped the small boy in his metal grave as they both sank into the depths of the Clyde. Horrible, twisting metal noises filled his ears as the box struggled to keep its rectangular shape, but with the enormous weight of excessive dirt deposit and added water pressure, drove strong forces into action, it triggered the tool chest to collapse inward. He held a palm on either side of the container in a futile struggle, where he hoped to stop the vessel from imploding, as it filled fast with a deluge of dirty brown water. His last effort would be to stare into the darkness of the strongbox which gripped him with a cruel and brutal fear.

The pirate ship was sinking further and deeper into the sediment which accepted the box and its small human contents willingly. Tommy's tiny lungs were near bursting as he grasped whatever air he could inhale. His struggles were ending. He would lose this battle. His last whimpering, unheard words were,

"Mum, Johnny-on-the-spot needs you."

Tommy has lost his ship at sea.

The Pirates of the Clyde have been defeated, and poor Tommy went down with his ship. Tommy was dead. Lost with his treasure. As he lay, within his vessel, silently on the ocean bed covered in tonnes of heavy sediment, a voice filtered through the murky waters.

"Do not fear death, my lad, you have a new home here in Davie Jones' locker!"

Donald awakened as if a trance-like state had overwhelmed him. He could hear the radio playing in the background, his senses appeared as if a dam had opened and everything flowed at a pace to re-energise and realise what magic held him in place. He moved his body and ventured from his seat to saunter towards the hallway where once the apparition of a small boy stood – the ghost boy that saved his life.

His mind did not work as it should. *Is this all a big crazy dream or is it real? It does seem real,* he thought. He spoke aloud, "OK, Tommy Shaw. I will help find you and bring you home to your family. I promise you."

A stretched-out arm grasped his black, knee-length coat, which hung from a nearby row of cast iron hooks that were wall mounted on a strip of mahogany. A few hats and jackets added to a full load of around seven items. He threw his arms into warm wool lined sleeves as he opened the heavy door which led to the cold stillness of the stairwell – a silence which would soon be erupted by a loud noise that echoed throughout the building as he slammed the door firmly behind him. A few neighbours would have jumped at the loud racket that interrupted their household chores.

He mumbled to himself as he left the apartment. The radio played soft American rock music.

Glasgow Cathedral
Present Day

This space was still recognisable to Donald. The old, grey lady of Glasgow, he imagined. The honorific cathedral, an 11th century edifice with the most beautiful example of the intricacies of mediaeval architecture that sits proudly on Castle Street. Many years of extreme weather and pollution have eroded the natural beauty of the Glasgow blonde sandstone which once would shine its presence on all that visited her, but in any era, she remained as beautiful as ever.

Jesus spoke, "Come with me, Donald. There is something I would like you to see."

Jesus walked towards descending steps that sat close to the nave and took the few footsteps down towards the basement level, where the lower church lies. On reaching the floor level, they stopped and stood near an ancient pillar, a long slim finger of Jesus pointed towards it which illuminated a bright light to show a strange, yet ornately carved text embedded in the stone.

"Tell me the message you read here, Donald."

Donald stared at the carved transcript, but his expression showed ignorance of what lay before him. The unusual square typeface looked more like graffiti than any resemblance to recognisable writing. Jesus spoke again as Donald stared at the pillar,

"That all of the eyes that have looked upon this text, and gave wonder to the originality, the importance, the ideology of it, or the theology some great minds offer, has had many scholars consider research into the script to be an academic disaster. Though others think the manuscript is a cypher that hasn't been revealed, and theories about the text's contents and origins abound. But everyone that views this carving sees it in individual ways. It forms a reason for any individual that seeks an answer or values truth. If you can't find truth where you stand, where else can you hope to find it?"

Donald bent his body further forwards to anchor his face near the carved shapes and hoped for a better and much-focussed view of the characters that drew closer to his gaze. He stared attentively, kept his focus on one letter shape among many others carved into the giant pillar. His attention stared central to the text. An intent look could not reflect his gaze from the vision he had no control. The letter characters moved around the pillar as if sand swirled in a mini tornado, the dynamic image before him, displayed letters from every world language, some of which he recognised, all spin into and out of view many times. Soon, he felt a surge of an enchanted force rip through powerful energy of light, and into his head.

His stance flew his body upright. Looking towards Jesus, he spoke, "I saw the words *Bonum Videre*, then I saw *Achchha Dekhen*, then possibly French words came into focus; *Voir le bien*. Then the shapes began to move randomly, shifting at pace around the pillar. It was then that I saw the jumbled letters form into English. It said, see the good. Yes, see the good.

"Does everyone that looks at this pillar see the same message?"

"Everyone is different, Donald. Your personal message is for your soul only through the doctrine of faith or belief, you have within you. It is all about particle intervention. And, just occasionally, these particles create a beautiful life that leads to a loving way beyond expectations. That is why I am here with you, Donald."

"You are part of a spiral of events that lead to a beautiful life. All souls originate from the same Divine Source, but there are many different pathways and paradigms, individual souls can take which shape their characteristics, undertakings, and even temperaments.

"Let me show you another part of this particle intervention which took place in 1982."

The sudden disappearance from the cathedral saw them stand once again as witnesses to a time long past in a Glasgow Street of 1982 which still looked familiar to Donald. A well-known street for him. He lived in the area and would have been around at this time. Yet, this was Duke Street, the longest road in Britain and he lived a few hundred yards away. *What happened here*? he thought, and could he remember an incident, however small it was, happen without him having knowledge? *Where was I today in 1982*? he wondered.

Donald looked around to see a typical busy day. People are working, shopping and going about their daily routine. He remembered the early 80s well. He had a Sinclair home computer, there were still only four TV channels, De Lorean cars were news headlines and being built-in Belfast, the Falklands war had begun and ended, Michael Fagan broke into the Queen's apartment in Buckingham Palace, and ET and Rambo (*First Blood*) were box office hits. His attention was broken by a woman screaming. It made most of the people in the area come to an impulsive standstill. Vehicles drew to a stop, and shopkeepers left their shops to join others on the pavement, just to see what created such an assembly. People pointed high in the air, heads stared upwards to the top tenement three storeys above the shops below which included a newsagent, a launderette, a bookmaker and a pub. Two dogs barked to add intrigue to the scene.

"My God, someone help the baby," an elderly woman screamed.

Other women held their hands tightly against their faces reluctant to participate in this grim incident, others looked away as a small baby, no older than two years old sat precariously on the edge of an open window.

"Where is the baby's mother?" a voice from the crowd shouted.

"For the love of God, someone, do something!" a middle-aged woman bawled aloud.

"Go back, go back inside," the group chanted.

"Go back, go get your mummy," another woman screamed.

"Someone phone 999," Donald heard himself murmur.

An energetic scream from the crowd of people was amplified with hi-pitch screams of horror and terror exhaled from the lungs of the cluster of adverse witnesses to this horrific, dreadful scene or the circumstances that came with it. The severe trauma would live with each witness forever. The crowd collectively screamed as the baby lost the safe position on the window ledge and fell forwards.

The baby plummeted downward at pace towards the pavement. Missing walls by inches as her body twisted and turned as it plunged downward. People turned away and could not bear witness to such a tragedy.

Donald, only a few feet away, watched the whole scenario unfurl before him. It seemed the baby fell through the warm June weather in slow motion. Golden locks of blonde curly hair ruffled through the air and her small tiny limbs spun wildly as if a doll fell from a great height. The baby fell fast, and Donald didn't want to see the outcome, yet with all his might, he could not take his focus from the event. He was a reluctant yet curious viewer.

As the baby neared death, a figure, a tall, slender-shaped young man flew at pace from a group of gathered people and lunged with force into space that people, notable, or unconsciously, had left vacant, knowing that the baby would ultimately land and die there.

His leap of faith looked very similar to a rugby star skimming through the air over trampled turf in a six-nation final to touch down the winning try.

His fierce, determined facial expression showed a willingness to react, or make some effort to save the baby's life, rather than be witness to such an appalling event. His outstretched arms gratefully accepted the full shape of the baby which he gripped with all his might, as both crashed to the ground and slid a few extra feet forwards, just missing a shop front wall, yet still managed to keep the child from contacting the surface. A few droplets of blood flowed from the young man's mouth having scraped his chin on the pavement and a bitten lip added to his only minor injuries.

Almost instantly, the baby burst into a chorus of high pitch screaming and tears poured from her eyes as the young man stood her upright close to where he lay. "A beautiful baby girl," was one woman's reaction on seeing the child standing erect, visibly healthy and alive on the space, destiny had thrown her a lifeline. Applause rang out from the crowd, and men and women alike made sure they either shook the hero's hand or pat his back to acknowledge his heroic deed. One senior man gave him a firm bear grip hug which suddenly proved to him that his action had brought more aches and pains than the adrenalin flowing through his body permitted him knowledge.

A woman, much younger than the hero, came screaming from the tenement building and forced her way through the gathered crowd. "My baby, my God, my baby." She rushed to the child and grasped her in a tightly held grip that it would undoubtedly hurt the child. But this young mother was scared and relieved to the point of collapse. The child looked content and happy to see her mother, and bystanders gave an acknowledgement that the young woman showed a positive motherly reaction towards the child, and presumably, she was indeed a good mother, that may have left the window open by mistake. It was June, to be honest, and the weather is sweltering. Things like this, however wrong, do sometimes happen. The baby girl looked so pleased to see her mother and would never fully understand the extent this ordeal would mean to her parent or the onlookers, yet a faint smile appeared just below her rosy-red cheeks which made every participant's, of this event, heartbeat slow to a more significant level. Attention was drawn towards the young woman, and her fortunate child with witnesses offering happy words of comfort as the young hero walked from the scene without notice.

"I can't believe that this happened. What a fantastic feat, the young man should get a medal. How on earth did he manage to save the baby's life?" Donald was keen to ask a few words.

Jesus didn't respond. The scene suddenly cleared as if erased from view and replaced with a similar version. Only a few vehicles were in the location. Some shop fronts had changed colour, a baker loaded his delivery van with bread and cakes, a postman delivered mail, people shopping and others waited patiently, in silence, for a local bus which was overdue. A few shopkeepers used long wooden poles, which had cast iron hooks protruded at one end to tug branded awnings down from a framed housing that stored the rolled fabric. A shopkeeper wore a blue bib apron threw a very hot, soapy, bucket full of water over the pavement near a shop front where a heavy brass broom swept away the previous night's litter. *Possibly, it was early morning,* Donald thought. It was the same street view but a different time!

His immediate was attention drawn towards a young man walking towards the area where he and Jesus stood. The man whistled. Donald's forehead creased in a frown-like manner as he got closer. His stare could not detract from the pacey frame of the jovial stranger ambling confidently in his direction. Did Donald recognise this young man? It all seems too real once again. This scene had a significant realm of reality linked to it, though he did not have one idea what was about to take place.

Then, in a moment of unexpected mystifying reality, a time he was unprepared for, happened – a woman's scream emanated from a top floor apartment he saw before him. He looked up, and in disbelief, saw a child, a slightly larger child than before, tumble from the window ledge where she once sat. Another person heard the same scream but acted differently by turning his stare from the awful scene he didn't want to witness. The whistling stranger too saw the child tumble then plummet at speed towards the solid surface of the tarmac pavement. But, as before, the stranger reacted in haste and made another leap of faith in another valiant attempt to save the baby. This time, however, no terror-stricken group gathered to see another extraordinary miracle or bear witness to such a rare phenomenon, the young man made another rugby style flight towards the baby. And like previously, he caught and held the child in a tight grip, and once again, saved her life. The sweet little soul whose name he didn't know looked helpless as she cried floods of tears. He placed her on her feet, and a local shopkeeper began to lead her to the safety of her baker shop and thanked the young man for this miracle. "This child has fallen from the same window twice now which is stranger than fiction, and beyond belief. It was around this time last year if my memory serves me correctly. How on earth can this happen?" the shopkeeper said with a rushed voice.

"Was it you that saved wee Jeanie before, are you an angel or something?" she added as the young man walked hurriedly from the scene. Wee Jeannie and the shopkeeper watched the young man fade from view. She took the child to the safety of the shop.

"A year to the day, the same small child fell from the same window saved by the same man and survived." Jesus looked at Donald and waited for him to respond.

"Is he an angel?"

"He is a man like you, Donald. Particle intervention or Vita de Vita, membris and membris which means, life is touching lives, and however strange or unbelievable a situation may look, this is, at times, a way life works."

Report

The police station on London Road, Bridgeton was relatively quiet when Donald stepped into the central reception area. A young woman sat on a wooden bench in the waiting area, held a handkerchief against her bleeding nose, two constables chatted as they left the building, wanted posters and drink driving awareness covered a small cork-framed noticeboard that sat at eye level behind the reception desk. The phone rang, the desk sergeant answered, "London Road Police Station, how can I help you?" He wrote several lines on a notepad with a small worn-down pencil about two inches in length, he finished the half minute phone call briefly. "I will pass on the message, sir, thank you."

Tearing the note from the pad, he turned and inserted it into a small wood frame docket where the name of Inspector Willie Lang stuck above the box. Donald observed that the embossed red tape with white writing that he had used in the past and recognised the familiar adhesive tape. Dymo came to mind.

The mid-aged sergeant laid the pencil down and laid both hands on his desk, he raised his head to look Donald in the eyes.

"How can I help you?"

"I would like to report a death, or a missing person, in fact, a boy. A missing boy!"

"A missing dead boy?" the sergeant said, confused. "And who is this missing dead boy and when exactly did he die?"

"He died in 1932 or thereabouts. I think."

"So how do you have information about this dead boy?"

"He visited me and gave me this note," he said laying the note on the desk near the officer.

The look on the face of the sergeant showed that time wasters would not be tolerated or given time to showcase nonsense, especially not on his watch. The officer lent forwards to Donald. "Consciously or unconsciously, are you trying to engage with me in a fruitless investment of wasting my energy, time or attention? Because if you are, you better leave now before I take you, or your story too seriously."

"No, sir, I am serious. This ghost boy appeared and gave me this piece of paper with his details on it." Donald didn't venture with further details about the previous night on the River Clyde as it would implicate him in the incident that he was sure the officer would at least have information and would more than likely ask questions. He wanted distance from last night's story. So, evasion was his initial thought.

He added further information to the officer.

"I live in the same house, and the ghost boy gave me this note and told me, he came into my dream to tell me where he can be found."

The officer read the letter aloud, "My name is Tommy Shaw. I live at 67a Bathgate Street in Glasgow. I want someone to save me. Tommy."

"So why has he waited 50 odd years to appear and to ask you for help?"

The officer's large dark eyes cut through Donald as he wondered how to answer correctly when a female voice chipped in unexpectedly.

"Check the missing records, that might help. I'm sure you will have records of missing people over the years," said the voice of the slender woman still seated. A blood-covered handkerchief muffled her verbal tones, but the sentences were clear and understood by both men.

The officer lent to the side slightly to see past Donald to gain a full view of the woman.

"Oh, I see, we have DS Jackie Reid from Maryhill CID that perhaps can assist with the case."

"She's not with me, officer. I can assure you," Donald offered in trepidation.

"I'm just saying, that's all," she offered further intrusion. "It's the sensible thing to do, at least, that's the way I would do it."

The officer turned his gaze to Donald.

"OK, I will have a clerk check this out. If, and I mean if, Any trace of this ghost or missing boy can be found, then we will be in touch."

"Thanks, officer. My name's Donald, Donald Forbes, and my address is 67A Bathgate Street Dennistoun."

"Fine," he said, using the small pencil to take note of his details.

"Thanks again, officer, your help is greatly appreciated." Donald turned and headed towards the exit, passed a young police officer entered the room, who in turn held the door open for Donald.

"I appreciate your help also." He grinned and raised his hand as a thank you gesture to the bloody nose woman. She gave a toothy smile in return. Donald left the building.

The desk officer shook his head in disbelief and was about to put the paper in the bin when a young officer entered through the front entrance.

"Morning, Sarge," he offered, and walked briskly past the desk heading to the corridor beyond when the desk sergeant interrupted his movement.

"I heard you were a hero last night. I thought you would have been off for a few days after the night you had."

"Not at all, Sarge, just a brief visit to the hospital and they signed me out. A few hours' sleep and back to the grind."

"Well, it's good to see you back fit and healthy, and what a great job you did last night by all accounts. It is always special when you save someone's life. Moreover, from the information I heard, then you deserve a medal. Well done!"

"Much appreciated, Sarge, but I don't think a medal is appropriate. I was doing my job," the young officer replied.

"Shaw!" the gruff well-toned vocals burst from officer Drysdale, stopped the young Bobby in his tracks.

"Sir," he said loud and clear.

"Maybe this is nothing, but since you have the same surname, it might be something, or it might be nonsense, and I think the latter, but what the heck."

The young constable looked bemused by the sergeant's intervention but didn't offer any words. He listened.

The officer held out the crumpled paper which he handed to the young constable and briefly told the story, he listened considerately and absorbed the tale fully. He stared at the note and kept his view entirely on it, as the officer chatted on about this weirdo that reported this peculiar account. Like a sudden shock wave that blasted energy through his whole body, he spoke three words which stopped the desk sergeant in his tracks.

"My great uncle!"

"You mean, you know this Tommy Shaw?" the dumbfounded officer offered.

"Yes, it's a family story. My father's uncle, Tommy, disappeared way back in the 1930s. He was just a young boy, he suffered from polio from an early age and wore callipers on his legs. He vanished without a trace."

His friends said they last saw him at play on the Glasgow Green before they headed home for tea, but after weeks of searching the Clyde, abandoned houses, sheds and lockups, there was never a trace of him. Even a poster campaign covered the city with no success, but still, no evidence of what happened to Tommy was ever discovered."

"But how can you be sure he is your great uncle?"

"The main fact is, Sarge, my father's uncle, Tommy Shaw, stayed in 67a, Bathgate Street in Dennistoun."

"Now that is a mystery, is it not," said the young woman still perched on the same bench. She grinned another toothy smile as both officers ogled her with disdain.

The Shipwreck

A few days earlier, PC Shaw had helped save a man from drowning in the Clyde. This additional mystery gave a fuller, more extravagant peculiarity to what was already a phenomenon beyond any reasonable understanding his mind usually had to deal with or any kind thought he could cope with.

It took a day or so for him to build up enough courage to visit the flat on Bathgate street. He had walked past the house on more than one occasion recently but didn't have the nerve to visit or even think about discussing Tommy Shaw with the present occupant. It just felt so weird and suitably strange, to seek information on a historical event, a landmark family mystery from many years ago, a mystery with a complete peculiarity that may or may not reside in the same house, the house where Tommy lived. Maybe the current occupant had knowledge of Tommy Shaw and was just weird enough to create this ghost story from some simple facts he had picked up, or perhaps he suffered from a personality disorder. Someone is playing games with the police. Possibly a raving lunatic! Just to waste police's time for the sake of it. A cry for help maybe.

PC Shaw, even as a young officer, had come across many strange and disoriented people in his short time policing in Glasgow. Watched a drunk hoover rain from large puddles in the middle of a street was just one of the crazy acts witnessed. Maybe this person is one of those. But a few minutes should lead him to a conclusion about whether to stay and listen to the man and his fanciful story or leave the premises. Try not to get overly involved. But, as a policeman, with a prospect to close a family mystery, curiosity got the better of him.

Today was the day he would try to meet the man with the incredible story. It was just after 6.30 pm, as he climbed the stairs to the top level. On the top landing, he saw the door face him. 67a embossed on metal numbers which sat top centre of the matte black painted door. PC Shaw was not in uniform; he dressed casually and thought a police uniform would not allow him full access to any relevant information. As a distant relative of young Tommy, the man may just open up more details. He thought this was the best way forwards.

The door took three fistfuls of loud banging. It opened after a second attempt, and a man similar in age to himself stood facing him. With a mouthful of foodstuff that lurked within his mouth, which he managed to swallow before speaking. "Yes, can I help you?" was Donald's offering.

"Hi, I'm an off-duty police officer, and I'm here to help with the disappearance of Tommy Shaw. I'm Ian Shaw." He offered his hand which Donald accepted, and shook. He added before Donald could react further, "Tommy was my great uncle! I got the information from my sergeant."

The door was thrown open, and Donald let him in.

Already locked in conversation, they walked towards the living room where Donald offered PC Shaw a can of lager taken from the sideboard, which he accepted. He pulled the ring pull, and a snap followed by a hissing sound gave a torrential frothy foam of beer, which PC Shaw supped from the lid. Pointing at the lager, lovely model printed on the side of the can, he smiled. "I've got Lorraine."

"I've got Erica," Donald said jokingly.

They chatted for over an hour as Donald explained his fairy-like story in graphic detail as he recalled with clarity, from the vivid dream, he imagined. An accurate description that gave the young officer an imaginative view as bright as the one Donald had. He now had information, information on which part of the Clyde was the site of the terrible accident and where young Tommy had lost his life. Facts on the boys and the games they played, the appalling weather that caused mudslides, a specific marker where his remains would lie, the time and date when Tommy died.

They soon began to plan a search and organise a team to work on recovering Tommy's remains. They both agreed that they could suffer the legal consequences later, but first and foremost, they will do their utmost to find young Tommy.

Glasgow Cathedral Present-Day

It was just after midnight, and Jesus and Donald sat once more on a pew near an ornate wooden pulpit. He saw the warm glow from the orange filter security lights that gave illumination to the interior of the church, and safe from the cold winter chill that lay outside.

"You remember the search very well?" uttered Jesus.

"I didn't have many memories from that time. Though having observed those scenes again, it brings memories back. We searched the river for Tommy's resting place, at the exact spot I saw in the hallucination. I honestly didn't believe we would find anything substantial to pinpoint Tommy. The box could have moved over the years. It could have rusted and fell apart and shifted with tides or weather."

"The search never took long, did it?"

"No, it was odd how it all happened. One of Ian's friends brought a manual winch, a hand winch he had anchored to a sufficiently large tree. A hook was attached to the wire winch cable, which was then thrown into the area I called 'the most likely area of probability', which we would trawl until it took hold of an object. If we felt a large object, the two small boats that sat in the river close by helped us in the search. They used long poles to test the size of the object that lay on the riverbed, prod the mud in an attempt to release Clyde's ill-gotten gains. We salvaged a bicycle, a hairdryer, an old type push lawnmower, a TV, a doll's pram among many objects. Then, I —" he stopped talking.

"You saw Tommy," said Jesus as Donald paused.

"Yes, surreal is not the word. I was about to throw the hook again back into the dark water when Tommy appeared visible. To me and no other. His head floated just above the water line, then both his arms came into view. He signalled for me to throw the wire towards him. I stared for a moment before I threw the hook and cable which, near as I remember, splashed into the water at the exact spot Tommy had appeared. My reaction was to tell the man on the winch to crank the handle fast and start to work the cable back to the spool. I knew then that the hook would have taken hold of Tommy's sea chest. It had to! I trusted Tommy to help at this point. He must make the hook catch a suitable part of the box so that we could raise it from its muddy grave. The strain was building, and two men were required to turn the ratchet as the hook had contacted an object. With a severe amount of weight being forcibly removed, they worked tirelessly, and Ian and I pulled the metal wire where we stood, with every effort, our strained muscles could give. The two boat crews were knocking the long poles into the river and hoped to dislodge the object of our search. Then, in an instant, a box flew from the slurry that held it in place, the boats collided and flung the participants back into the centre thwart wooden seat. I released the cable, as did Ian, and the ratchet drew the heavy object upward towards the riverbank. This wrench, believably, could move loads ranging from a few hundred pounds to several tons. So removing the box up onto the bank would be no problem whatsoever.

"As the box left the solitude of the murky Clyde, muddy water dripped continually as it came up over the edge of the bank and settled close to where we stood. We knew instantly that this was the lost tomb of young Tommy Shaw.

"The strange thing was, that the cable wrapped tightly around the box and the hook locked in place around the wire, was a single vertical hitch, which would be impossible without the use of a diver having unobstructed access to the box, but no one mentioned this peculiarity, and I didn't offer this information."

After they opened what remained of the rusty old box, both Ian and Donald felt relief, but sadness and sorrow soon filled their deep emotions, even though closure to the missing boy was near. Their search assistants, mostly retired police officers, gathered around the strongbox, and religiously paid respect and bowed their heads. Donald offered a few words of condolence, as all in attendance mumbled a soft-spoken Amen.

Ian Shaw took an extra measure and phoned a colleague at the station soon after, who set in motion legal requirements of such a discovery. The CID (Criminal Investigation Department) appeared on site to make an initial and brief assessment of the find, and reviewed the full story by Ian and Donald.

The coroner's office took charge of Tommy's remains and had a forensic anthropologist study his bones, to gain a view of skeletal abnormalities which would determine a cause of death potentially, historical distress such as broken bones or pathological processes, as well as diseases, could assist in identifying any victim. After examining the cold case of missing children, the CID was more than happy to define the human remains as Tommy Shaw, the metal callipers and remnants of clothes and boots, and the specific area of discovery was evidence enough to put closure on this case, noted as death by drowning.

A few days later, and with many documents signed and stamped, the remains were released to Ian and his family who had thankfully gained permission for young Tommy to be laid to rest with his parents. It was a quiet moment of contemplation to all in attendance at the quiet graveside at Glasgow Necropolis Cemetery. The occasion brought joy to the family, however gruesome and terrible this tormented event had taken Tommy's short life, though now, it finally brought an end to the mystery of young Tommy Shaw's disappearance.

Occasionally, a lone visitor would attend Tommy's resting place and place a small sprig of heather at the base of the Shaw family headstone, always with the nautical verse attached.

1998

December 19th, 1998, Saturday, Glasgow City Centre.

It started raining. It was 2.40 am on Saturday morning, and Donald was ready to head home after a very long demanding shift. The last fare, a middle-aged couple, argued non-stop, from St Vincent Street to Hillhead. *God, why do I do this job,* entered his tired concentration and his deliberate attitude to avoid confrontation, he just let them get on with it. If no physical violence takes place or his taxi becomes a marital battleground, he could live with it. Most nonsense in his cab, though not welcome, could at least be tolerated. Taxi drivers are generally accustomed to this scenario, especially when alcohol is involved. Though, after he received a prompt payment in full, with a few pounds extra in a tip, he encouraged a goodnight to the disorderly man as he slowly walked behind his wife towards their home, only to receive a loud, "Yeah, and up you arsehole!" in a heated reply. Charming!

The drive was relatively quiet at this time of morning and especially this time of year, with only a few stragglers headed home from Xmas parties or nightclubs. A detour to his usual taxi rank near George Square would be his last move of the shift he planned. But, for some unknown reason, whatever thought came to mind, to make such a call and contradict his straightforward idea, he turned off the regular route, and what would be the shortest course. His mind could not fathom why he suddenly changed direction. Imagined if he had a new-fangled Satnav as some taxis do, it would be repeated a sentence, with an irritating computer voice, "About turn at the next exit."

His cab turned left from West George Street, drove up Hope Street heading towards Cowcaddens. *A bizarre route, to say the least,* he repeated to himself.

The city was soundless and deserted as he approached Sauchiehall Street junction as it crawled to a stop at red lights. *There are no pedestrians,* he thought but wait he did. Then, in a single flash, a movement caught his eye, he thought he saw a figure of a young woman, pulled unwillingly into a small lane just off Hope Street. Donald instantly knew the path, it was Renfrew Lane which led from Hope Street to Renfield Street.

Did he see this?

The lights changed to green, and he moved his taxi faster than usual and stopped abruptly, and parked, just before the entrance road. He left the comfort and safety of his heated cab, and ventured towards the narrow path. He saw no one at this point. Before him, the alley had a multitude of garbage bins, a small skip full of builder's waste, a shopping trolley and rubbish of all sorts littered the walkway – but no visible sight of anyone could be made, far less a young woman. "Hello!" he shouted. "Anybody there?" He felt stupid but spoke again, "Hello, is there anybody there?"

Then, at that moment, a faint scream was heard, a muffled cry, an inaudible cry for help. *What should I do? Phone the police? Shit, what do I do?*

A serious glance towards the builder's skips to look for materials in them, gave many options for weapons if he needed them. Yes, he thought he would need them. And it didn't take long till he found some. A large piece of wood or a chair leg was chosen and a decent length of the steel bar. He placed one in either hand and strolled forwards, but steadily dodging litter, and observed every space he passed. Trying to look beyond the mixture of red, blue, green and grey coloured plastic rubbish containers, hoping to see any person hiding in wait for his arrival. The left-sided wall before him had piles of large pallets propped against it, and a high steel and aluminium extractor unit clung insecurely to the wall where a chimney ran from ground level to the roof. It stuck out a few feet and could easily conceal hidden foes; though it didn't. Sweat dripped from his forehead over his eyes, even though the temperature was around 1°C. His nerves were entirely out of control, his arms were visibly shaking, his lower lip bled as his top teeth were pinched on it and his neck showed Goosebumps. But he kept moving onward, checking every nook and cranny as he continued. He remained vigilant but unsure of what lay ahead.

Halfway along the alley, still walking apprehensively, there, before him, he noticed a concealed locked security doorway to his right that receded a few feet back into the building. It was a dark area and could hide a few people. His eyes grew weary as he continuously stared at this spot, but he was sure of some movement in the darkness, just a slight shift of light change which his eyes perceived, confirmed to his senses that this was the place he was searching. As he got closer to the door, about ten feet in distance, his eyes accustomed to the dull light. Staring continually at this space, dark figures of two men and a young woman (who was held tightly against the metal-framed door), with one man covering her mouth with a large, steady hand came into view. The other, a stocky built man of around 5'10", walked a foot or so forwards from the shadowy enclosed entrance, just enough steps to shine even duller streetlights on him and for Donald to see him clearer. He spoke with no fear or showed any concern about his presence, "Do yourself a big favour and fuck off, pal," his voice growled in a loud guttural tone.

Donald stood still, focussed his view past the ugly man, the one that wanted to do him harm, towards the young woman, he now saw wriggling in a desperate fight to escape. Her struggles got her nowhere, every move made her weaker and less capable of winning the battle. Her struggle was futile, hopeless against her attackers. Under the annoyingly dim light that shone in the alley, Donald saw the young woman stare back at him in fear. The whites of her eyes were bright, shone like a beacon, pulsated fear towards Donald. A cry for help, she pleaded for someone to take the pain away, an angel, a guardian angel, anyone with a kind soul.

Suddenly, with excessive force, the young woman was thrown back into the darkness of the entrance, and a high pitch scream of fear left her mouth as the stranger that held her, threw a punch that was hard enough to knock a man over, far less the frame of a helpless young woman, land square on her face. She collapsed instantly, but the limp body was held upright by her assailant as a hunter seized his prey. The other man still stood in the same spot and faced Donald, smiling, he spoke again, "I told you to fuck off." He turned and walked back into the entrance in the belief that the passive helper would wet his pants and run for his life.

Time itself, sometimes over-elaborates circumstances, the more you think about it, the less assured you become. Whether to make a move or when it is required to do so, is always the question that appears in a situation like this. But move he did. A confident leap of faith at pace, followed by a heavy blow from his raised right arm, brought the solid wooden chair leg down on the large man's head. A second strike followed immediately, and it dropped the aggressor to a pile of human debris that added to the other worthless trash that littered the alley. This new collection of ground refuge didn't talk either, but it did make a groan or two as it confirmed a bond with the wet soggy ground. The other man, whom Donald now saw in the light of the alley, was smaller, much smaller, a little ugly face was his first impression. A little aggressive, arrogant evil type, he guessed. A small rat figure wore a black baseball cap punctuated with a white brand logo embossed on the front peak, and dark bomber type jacket zipped closed under his chin, and an excessive stagger of self-assurance made him saunter a few feet towards Donald, look eager and confident.

"You think you're a fuckin' hard man?" he dropped the girl in a bundle where she lay static, he approached slowly with what looked like a knife, held firmly in his right hand, wielding it in striking motions towards Donald. He smiled and moved the blade in a cutting motion which looked more like a ritual dance than a serious assault, or attempted murder or murder which made Donald even more scared. "Come on, you fucking prick. See how you fancy some of this." He slashed the knife towards Donald which made him sway backwards away from the blade. An action that happened several times.

Donald watched the man's movement closely, he stepped back responsively from every lunge the unscrupulous rat made, yet he drew closer step by step, and as the switchblade prodded for a body to puncture. Donald reacted, he felt he had to, and threw the piece of wood at the man's body which made him recoil and stagger slightly, that set him off-guard. Donald used this moment to swing with all his power, swing the metal rod down towards the attacker, and luckily, it struck him solidly in the centre of his head, just around the cap logo, making him fall hard to the ground. Dropped out cold as he laid motionless on the slippery damp cobbles near his companion. *Like a ton of bricks*, phrase entered his mind but move fast from this area was his prime objective. As he stepped over the two attackers, he struck them powerfully on the legs with the metal bar to make sure they would not get up or continue this horrible experience they were intent completing. A slight groan from one aggressor was heard, but no movement detected from either. Maybe further strikes were not called for, but these thugs would kill if they were awake or responsive. He was thankful, they were inactive and unresponsive.

The young woman was disoriented, but conscious, possibly drugged. He had witnessed young women in the past being doped with a cocktail of illegal drugs and her appearance certainly gave him rise to his belief that this was the case. More than likely drugged by the two attempted rapists. Other than her shabby demeanour, she looked as though he arrived at the perfect time, even her shoulder bag still strapped around her neck. A few cuts and bruises on her face and ripped clothing were the only visible damage, but police and hospital was his next action, as soon as he got to the safety of his taxi. Getting the girl to safety was his priority.

Donald carried the girl and hoped a police officer or street camera picked up on this. He knew too well, as all public transport licenced drivers did that City Watch monitored all cameras for the city centre at Stewart Street police station. Where was the response? A taxi driver left his cab unattended on a night which was void with people? Plainly, someone saw a young woman abducted and pulled into a dark, poorly lit alley by two men would ignite a reaction. Surely, it would! Those camera operatives are brilliant at their job, and he knows first-hand how good they are. One passenger, months back, had refused to pay his fare and kicked the cab door repeatedly, and set about abusing the black bodywork of his taxi. And before he could radio for help, a police squad car arrived rapidly, arrested the argumentative drunk, and he spent a night in the cells – and charged, of course. The judge granted Donald costs and his vehicle repairs were at paid for, and by the idiot that did the damage.

Donald tried speaking to the young woman and told her he would take her to the hospital and call the police on en route. However, still weary with the drug effect, she shouted with as much lung effort her body could provide, she cried out, "No!" as loud as her body gave her access to a semi-conscious state. "Take me home, please. Take me home," and her frail vocal effort made her body limp and she passed out. Donald had drunk passengers in his cab many times, and on some occasions, made severe attempts to exit the moving taxi. At least this time, he could sit the young woman upright and tighten the seat belt suitably to hold her weak body in situ.

Back into the comfort of his driver's seat, he felt slightly ill at ease searching the young woman's handbag, but he did need to know where she lived, and any identification at this point would most certainly help. An occasional glance into the mirror showed the young woman reclined safely and enclosed securely in position. His luck was in, a driving license from her purse confirmed the face and the address noted her home locality. He spoke to himself, "74, Green Lawn Crescent, Dougalston, Milngavie. Perfect. Near the golf course, I have played there many times." He turned to face the sleeping young woman and spoke, "Let's get you home, young lady."

The taxi started, the engine pushed into gear as it moved forwards into the early morning rain, in the new direction of Milngavie.

Unknown to Donald, the street cameras in the Hope Street area stopped for over an hour. As he drove out of the city centre, they began working again. A bug in the system was the conclusion, but not the truth.

It took around twenty minutes to arrive at the destination. Some days it could take 40 minutes, depending on the traffic, but at this time of the morning, it was a leisurely ride.

The Olive Man

Two strangers, the stinking rat and his repulsive co-conspirator, the vile pig – the black-hearted twosome – stood unsteadily on their feet in the cold night air which blew blustery through Renfrew Lane. Both physically shaken and hurt by their recent ordeal at the hands of Donald Forbes.

The small rat was vocal with his partner and verbally abused him as they took uneasy steps towards Renfrew Street.

All this action was closely watched by a solitary crow that sat perched high above the ground on a ledge of the Pavilion Theatre. It viewed every step both men made. It watched every sullen movement with precise accuracy. Momentarily, it unexpectedly swooped silently to the ground where it landed softly close-by the criminals, where it transformed into a human being; a man, a man dressed in black. A tall, elegant man with wavy jet-black hair and olive coloured skin stood his ground as the imminent deviants approached him. Both evil men froze dead in their tracks when the olive man came clear to view. They feared the intruder! They knew this stalker!

Two unscrupulous, depraved minds were immobile. They remained motionless, speechless, reckless, shameless, but consciously aware of their imminent fate. They spoke no words, but the look of fear in their eyes showed much terror.

The olive man raised his right arm with his palm facing both men and spoke a phrase which sounded adenoidal, where some of the sounds seemed to come through his nose. As one would expect from a half bird, half human being. His voice was deep and intense as a Latin phrase boomed towards the trembled faces of the unemotional figures, which accommodated evil-doers:

"Puvis et umbra sumus, fiat lux." (We are but dust and shadows, let there be light.) A flash of concentrated white light lit the area. The alley became daylight for a few seconds or more. Faint screams were heard from the wicked souls. If they had souls? Gone! Both gone! Evaporated into tiny fragments of dark waste that were dispersed by a cold wind that suddenly blew as it propelled its purgative air through the dark dreich alley. The fresh air eradicated the wicked despair that had dwelt here. The olive man took several steps and rapidly morphed back into the familiar shape of a crow. A solitary crow flew deep into the darkness of the night. Faded, undisturbed, into a distant cloud covered moonlight that hung over the city of Glasgow.

Violet Goes Home

The events of today had taken a severe toll on Violet's moral strength. Values, which she held dear, had ever so slightly crumbled. Though moral support from an outsider gave her regained hope and a clear view on the principles of virtue that she held dearly. A brave stranger laid his life on the line to tackle evil perpetrators from committing sin by taking her life. Both men intended to subdue her beliefs and violate her moral code and practices, break a young woman that emitted a strong sense of empathy and justice to the world, and unwavering faith would be a perfect act. Evil was ready to destroy the goodness of her soul.

Thankfully, her prayers had been answered and God sent an angel. A human angel.

After a short journey, Donald arrived at her home. Following a quick period of introductions and stories explained, and a few hot drinks consumed – her aged grandmother, Jessie, decided Violet needed much rest and she headed directly, without much persuasion, to her warm, welcomed bed.

The sun had risen, and birds could be heard singing as Donald sat and listened to a story that was beyond fiction and would possibly stretch the imagination of any top writer. He felt welcomed in her home and entirely accepted by Jessie, who in turn, identified Donald as a man of trust and held strong faith, and she saw a bright aura shine around him.

She trusted him unequivocally.

Jessie Brook was a retired teacher. She explained how tragedy brought hope to her life at a time when all seemed lost.

It was 1982 when she first received terrible, yet compulsory, factual and disturbing news from Glasgow's constabulary (and not information any parent would ever wish to hear) her only child, Eva, was dead.

Her daughter's body had been discovered by a group of children while playing in an empty tenement block. Initially, the police thought it was another drug overdose. Just another death from illegal substance abuse.

Jessie told her story,

"A few days before Eva's death, she took the baby to a close friend and asked if she could look after her until she sorted her situation out. A condition she told her friend which was severe and dangerous, and the baby had to be safe for the next few days, at least until she could plan a move away from Glasgow. Her friend didn't know too much of the circumstances but did say Eva looked scared and agitated, and not her usual self.

"Oddly, she told her friend to keep the baby hidden and avoid two strangers. Two men, two evil men, but she didn't add any information to this fact.

"Eva wanted her baby safe and insisted that if she didn't return by the weekend, her friend was to contact me and hear the full story. But this is where that story takes a nefarious and sinister diversion. After a complete autopsy, the pathologist discovered a forced needle injection at the nape of her neck which had penetrated her brain. A lethal dose of impure heroin flushed into her body along with a cocktail of benzodiazepines, valium and Rohypnol, which I discovered is a date rape drug. A copious amount of alcohol was also found in her system. Her body had been beaten severely. She had been kept prisoner.

"It soon became apparent that she had been tortured, raped then murdered!

"When I heard both you and Violet's stories, my heart missed a beat. Two strange men, once again, appearing close to my family, and intent on doing harm. I don't have answers, the police never traced either man. They kept the case open, but all these years later, there still is no justice brought on the perpetrators."

Donald was more than willing to listen. Both felt comfortable in each other's company. Jessie continued,

"What I'm about to tell you, Mr Forbes, may or may not be accepted or believed by you. I knew too well that my daughter could not be Violet's mother. When Eva was sixteen, just a schoolgirl, she fell pregnant. This was a very trying and traumatic time for our family. My husband, Jack, was suffering ill health, and had the first of three heart attacks and was dead within three months. I was left with continual worry and anguish that came with fear, a fear I had never experienced before, as my only child suffered deep depression. But I remained firm for the sake of my daughter.

"We both agreed that abortion, for the benefit of Eva's mental health, was morally acceptable, and with the state of her mind at that time, it was the best way forwards.

"Eva, my sick child, had an abortion, an abortion that caused severe damage to her physical and mental health. The surgical procedure had dreadful complications. During the operation, Eva's womb was severely damaged, so you see, Donald, there would never be a possibility of Eva giving birth.

"At this time, her mental health problems deteriorated fast. Within a year, Eva had left home. Only on my birthday or Christmas, a card would arrive with a small note informing me of her well-being. Not a visit or a phone call. Never a hug or a kiss.

"So, you see, I found all this disconcerting and confusing to accept. It was not the picture I would paint of my daughter being involved with drugs. I couldn't allow my feelings to believe her involvement in anything criminal or unpleasant. She was a good girl. But I knew, my priorities had to focus on baby Violet."

She paused as she gained the strength to continue and her story moved forwards a few years.

"When Violet started school, her first day, in fact, and bear in mind, she was just short of her 5th birthday, she cut paper hearts of many different colours, and gave one to each of her classmates and one to her teacher. On each heart, there was a word. She had used five words. Hope, joy, respect, blessed and love. She was a beam of light, Mr Forbes. From the day I first held her in my arms, I knew this baby was full of love and light, whatever you want to call it. For want of a better term, she was a little angel. A pure soul! This never changed, she would attract all types of animals and birds like a guru or Doctor Doolittle. Violet would sit in the garden on a summers' day, and have butterflies perch on her head and arms.

"Birds would appear on the ledge of her bedroom window. One day a crow arrived and has been a regular visitor ever since."

Jessie Brook paused before continuing.

"At first, I could not understand why my daughter would leave Violet with a friend, gave suspicious information to keep her baby safe, be in fear of two unknown strangers, and had the fortitude and strength of character to look for a way out. That was more like my daughter. Not an abuser of drugs or alcohol, or any form of narcotic addiction. But someone that wanted her child safe, for whatever the reason she had placed on her, she acted with good intentions of putting Violet first."

Donald smiled as he listened to Jessie Brook's incredible story. He wondered if the round pair of glasses that she stared through had a similar effect to the lenses Jesus had shown him.

The old lady talked more,

"As Violet grew older, I wanted answers for myself as much I needed the truth for her. I decided to do a DNA test on us both. It was done and posted, and I waited patiently for the results. Results that never arrived. You see, Mr Forbes, after I posted the saliva samples, later that day, as I sat in my garden, I suddenly moved to a place called Nostalgia. A place that gave answers, a place of truth and love. I travelled through time, met people I became close to, discovered knowledge that had veracity. I met you, Donald. Watching, as my granddaughter falls from a tenement building. You saved my granddaughter twice, and tonight you saved her a 3rd time."

Donald lowered his eyebrows that creased his forehead, but he didn't speak.

"When I visited Nostalgia, I met my late husband and a few other kind souls. You see, Donald, on my visit to Nostalgia, I was informed that evil would persist in attempts to abuse and oppress Violet on every occasion. I was to keep her safe, safe until she reached the age of 20. Evil was bent on damaging Violet's pure soul and endeavour to break her spirit every way possible. All in a view to stopping her from becoming angelic. Her future self would light a bright light over many unfortunate people and give hope to generations. So, as you see, I knew of your existence long before we met, and knew you would be the man that would bring my granddaughter home safe. Even though tonight, I prayed with extreme intensity, my head ached, I prayed with all my heart for Violet's safe return. And thankfully, you brought Violet home, just as I had been foretold."

Donald had no answers, nor did Jessie. But together, they journeyed the same route, bonded to the same cause and working to save a young girl's life for the benefit of a better future.

"What were you told at this place Nostalgia?" Donald asked.

"I was told that no DNA result would be received. But I was told the truth. An unimaginable truth. Beyond the realms of my belief or understanding."

The old lady paused.

"Donald, Violet is unique. So unique, in fact, she has my maternal DNA, but no paternal Y chromosome.

"DNA tests, I had previously believed, showed both maternal and paternal sides of the family tree. In Violet's case, however, the Y chromosome, which is inherited from the father's side, will never be detected. The girl is divine. Maybe not heavenly or celestial, but indeed a gift from God. That is the way I see it," she further added.

"I was to raise Violet in a loving home, let her express her beliefs and show her inspirational soul in purity, holiness and innocence. I became her grandmother and guardian."

Within a moment, the conversation stopped, and the day ended abruptly. Donald had moved again.

11.45 PM Christmas
Eve Present-Day

The sun had long set and darkness had fallen, and heavy, moist wet snow painted an honourable festive scene on the streets of Dennistoun.

Alone, a solitary crow sat perched on a tall, sodium vapour lamppost that gave a deep, warm feeling to the cold biting night as it emitted a superfluous orange glow that lit a large area. It was the leading light in this part of Bathgate Street. Sitting on the street corner of Reidvale Street, it illuminated the full junction and gave added security to a few snow-covered vehicles parked nearby. The bird sang a fantastic song, a song no one would ever expect from a large carrion crow, but it sang beautifully yet no one was near to receive such a captivating melody. It fluttered its wings to remove excess snow that had built-up on its body. A full vocal squawk from the crow echoed through the stillness of the relatively calm evening, after yet another whole-body shake, more snow was dispersed from its bright blue, black plumage – in preparation, as it leapt from its roost to swoop upward towards the window ledge of Donald's apartment, its destination. As it gained a foothold, looking through a small unblemished bright area free from condensation, on the window corner, saw people enjoying themselves.

People were eating, drinking and chatting like birds, orderly sitting at a large square table while listening to music and having Champagne regularly administered to each glass. They wore funny paper hats and blew paper trumpets that rolled into a coil, then unrolled, when the humans blew into it, producing a horn-like squeak and unearthly type of noise.

Not a bird song by any means!

A tree with strange lights sat in the far corner of the room. Lights regularly pulsated and twinkled in and out. A small figurine of a woman with large pink wings sat on top of the tree. She was smiling. Many boxes of different shapes and sizes sat at the foot of the tree. The crow found this strange. It turned its gaze away from the window as it flew off into the night.

Fifty yards or so, from Donald's third floor apartment, somewhere along Reidvale Street, standing by green painted metal railing that acted as a security barrier for the rail line that lay a few feet beyond stood a lone figure. A man, a senior man, dressed head to toe in black. A long coat covered most of his frame and a scarf nestled around his neck, and a Fedora hat rested tight on his head which included a copious amount of grey hair extending over cashmere neckwear. Plumes of blue smoke from a large Cuban cigar, or better still, a Gurkha's Black Dragon cigar filled the air around him. The Black Dragon includes a global mix of ageing tobaccos underneath its vibrant leafy casing. At £110,000 a box or £1,100 per cigar, Gurkha's Black Dragon cigars are both ludicrously costly and respected. This gentleman was rich.

The man kept his attention on Donald's apartment. He was in deep thought. He continued his stare towards the warmly lit room at the top of the apartment block.

It was Christmas Eve, and Christmas was close. The man remained in the same position for over an hour, with not one person or neighbour paying attention to him. Freezing temperatures persistently gnawed at him, yet he continued to stand in the same place. Occasionally shaking the snow from his frame with a jerk or two, but mainly kept his organised view towards Donald's apartment.

The conversation filled the small apartment; laughter was an essential part of the evening's mix. It was jovial and cheerful.

It was then that Donald made an impulsive move to look out the living room window. He did so without realising why or instinctively understood any reason behind the move – for no other purpose than a spontaneous action of doing something – by looking out the window. He took a few steps from the table and walked towards the sash-framed window that gave a full view of Reidvale Street.

He moved his hand over the glass to remove cold condensation which gave a more unobstructed view of a snowy outside world. Immediately, his eyes were drawn to the lone figure, the unfamiliar person in the snow, an oddity of a stranger that looked so peculiar in circumstances of this moment. Donald kept a continual focus on the figure.

His guests bellowed questions on the severity of the weather from behind him and expected a report of some kind, but he gave no response, his mind was engrossed as he watched the figure blow blue smoke into the night air.

The party continued behind him.

A car, a large black car, in fact, a limousine of substantial size moved silently into Bathgate Street and drove slowly through the snow leaving behind imprinted tyre marks. It slowed, and brake lights illuminated the area further as it parked near the outsider. A tall figure, also dressed in warm black clothing, stepped from the driver's position. He also wore a hat, a chauffeur's cap, he walked to open the rear door and stood patiently for his guest – the engine was running. The stranger took a few short steps, stopped before entering, stubbed the last portion of the expensive cigar in the snow and placed a twisting foot on it to confirm this, then joined the driver in the heated vehicle. Donald watched the conclusion to the scene as the man in black stepped into the car. It remained static for a minute or so before moving slowly forwards, where it disappeared elegantly into the snow filled night.

Unexpectedly, a crow plunged from above Donald's viewpoint which startled him and made him step back from the window. His returned stare readjusted to the outside light momentary where his regained vision saw the bird fly from his apartment through the sheets of cold white snow as it followed the car. He smiled at the surrealism of this experience. The orange glow from the streetlight flickered, then went out. It was now a dark street with lots of white snow producing more layers over previous solid layers. Snow soon covered the undisturbed tyre marks. *A beautiful scene if ever there was one,* he thought.

"Merry Xmas!" reverberated from behind him which made him turn his attention back to his guests. A wall clock chimed twelve. Paper trumpets blew annoyingly, party poppers banged and gave cracking noises as small plastic bottles shaped projectiles blasted heaps of confetti streamers over everybody in attendance and more than enough coloured paper fell into their charged glasses.

It was Christmas, and the party continued.

Nostalgia

Every distinct move Donald found himself making, whether it added to an extraordinary journey of revisiting his past or seeing the life that had long disappeared from memory, would be held in perpetuity, tightly in the grip of history itself, all of which were unique moments in his solitary life. Each expedition still made him surprised and scared to a certain extent. First appearing in one place or another, moving in milliseconds gave him a colourful picture of a multi-observance that he now understood ever more efficiently. It was a sample of his early life which had developed over many years. A snap of time, transportation of a living being to another realm, to witness vanished memories was way beyond belief. Even though his mind could not truly understand the magnitude or the scale of these actions – he knew he was one of the main characters involved in this beautiful story and felt the kooky connection was justified in some peculiar way.

It was three am.

Instant travel was slightly tolerable to him as he found himself standing on a railway platform, facing a Glasgow subway train which he instantly recognised as an exhibition hall piece and not an actual working train or part of any moving rolling stock. There was no sign of Jesus, just him, standing, staring at a non-moveable empty object. A sign above the mock-up display train said, 'Next stop Nostalgia'. His captivation of the moment suddenly grasped his attention, when a small man, dressed in full train conductor uniform of former times, appeared next to him which made him jerk with fright. The dour-faced conductor looked as though he had dissolved from a period drama to spend a few moments in the allocation of Donald's life. His Kepi-style cap (which was the regulation type of head ware that both the Union and Confederation armies wore during the American Civil War) sat fully on his head. The word *Conductor* embroidered on the front portion of the hat, his small lean body engulfed in an oversized 12-button great coat which swept over his knees to reveal a small part of black trousers which had several layers turned up over his black shiny hobnail boots. He certainly looked like he wasn't a man to tolerate much messing around!

A button on his left breast held a bulky yellow enamelled badge with black script writing, donating the text 39T. A leather satchel firmly strapped over his left shoulder, with the bag pressing tightly against his right hip, which he opened and produced an envelope-sized card. A walrus, untrimmed moustache covered most of his lower face moved upwards, then downwards, yet no mouth movement could be detected, though precise words emitted from him. He spoke and was heard, but no sign of his mouth, which lay under a bristle of long facial hair. Donald found this meeting somewhat amusing.

"This is for you, Mr Forbes," the voice of a proud transport official bellowed as he clicks a ticket punch over the invitation that threw a small, unusable disc of paper to the ground. "Done and dusted, enjoy your day, sir," he said, forcing the card in Donald's direction.

Donald stared openly towards the card. Which read:

Admits 1

You are cordially invited to

Nostalgia

for a sentimental journey

Please board the Balmanno Brae Express

Glasgow

Enjoy the ride!

The Inspector

*Admits 1. You are invited to **Nostalgia**. For a sentimental journey of emotion. Please board Belmanno Brae Express Glasgow.*

Enjoy the ride! The Inspector.

By looking at the card, he hadn't noticed the conductor leave the area. He simply vanished into thin air. Donald instinctively headed in the direction of the unmovable mock tube train, wondering where his next voyage would take him. *A beautiful train*, he thought, *though it is an exhibition model. The 39T is a restored trailer carrier which dated back to 1898 and built by Hurst Nelson of Motherwell, and is now an exhibition piece at the Riverside Transport Museum.* Donald seemed to know all this relevant information as it rushed through his mind giving him personal details about the subway train he was about to board.

The only knowledge he had of spotting or recognising any other locomotive on earth would be The Flying Scotsman, and even that would be a pure guess.

He took a seat in the empty carriage and sat close by a substantial piece of glass that partitioned half of the train.

Almost immediately, a soft, yet forceful voice emanated from somewhere close by, though he couldn't pinpoint where. A glance around the subway car looking for speakers didn't shed much light on the subject either. It was a man's voice and sounded similar in tone to that of the inspector he had just met.

"Dear passenger, I would like to take this opportunity to thank you for travelling with Balmanno Brae Express today. Just remember that on departure in a few moments, please follow the signs for Nostalgia where you can gain entry with the unique invitation you are carrying. Enjoy your day!"

The door hissed closed with a sudden injected flood of pressurised air. Then the train, the display train, started to proceed forwards. Moving slowly at first then building up to a fast-accelerated pace. Donald being shunted around uncomfortably in his seat as the carriage flew onward. It was a pleasant experience. Sitting in a subway locomotive all by himself with no sullen commuters voicing opinions, with straight faces stuck deeply in daily newspapers, people with colds, sneezing or coughing and spreading the disease to all commuters, or others moaning about the weather or work or just the quiet passenger catching another few minutes' sleep. So this experience was indeed a moment to savour. It all felt like a hyper-reality experience or a multi-sensory magical illusion. A theme park simulator was the nearest familiar thrill, he imagined, could match this exhilarating ride.

But this was greater than any theme park ride. A place like this is a museum mock-up, for God's sake! No actual rail line network or physical excavated tunnels encircled under Glasgow city centre were here, it was make-believe. No tube stations lay ahead. How can this be real? His mind wandered through many possibilities, to attempt acceptance of this complicated reality.

Donald remained seated as his fictional journey continued, the train flew forwards and kept running fast, hurtling through mysterious black tunnels, passing non-existing stations. Station names that seemed far-fetched and unusual to Glasgow or any place he knew.

Names that appeared in the light as the train slowed, but never stopping, as it hurtled through each secret location. Names like Stirling Street, Canning Street, Jail Square and East Union Street among many that Donald watched with a baffled look as he remained to wait for his destination.

After minutes, possibly ten or more, which was much slower than he expected. Especially when every jump in time he made of late had been instantaneous.

The tube train slowed effortlessly to a stop. An oversized wall sign promoting the word, Nostalgia, came into view as Donald walked towards the carriage door as it again hissed more pressurised air to burst open. He expected to hear the usual train communitive rail protocol when leaving a train carriage: *Please mind the gap when alighting the train*. But he didn't. Not another soul in sight or no voiced message boomed from any invisible tannoy speaker, it was peaceful yet surreal. His mind told him that this place was so inconspicuous, it reminded him of a boat tour he took on holiday in Cyprus last year when, with the aid of powerful binoculars, he could view the deserted area called Varosha which is an abandoned southern quarter of the Cypriot city of Famagusta. Not a person in sight, just seabirds resting on derelict buildings. Every structure was uninhabited for many years. Before the Turkish invasion of Cyprus in 1974, it was a popular tourist area of the city. When the inhabitants fled, their possessions remained. Newspapers were left open on tables. Bottles of alcohol left on bars tops. New cars sat in showroom windows, grocer shops stocked with food. Most people thought they were parting for a few hours, so literally walked out with the clothes on their backs. A ghost town is full of memories, abandoned properties and void of life with every empty building with a story to tell. Deserted and left for the elements to destroy the remaining infrastructure, year after year and allowed to depreciate, as nature herself decides the outcome of a once lively, vibrant and colourful city.

A large Nostalgia sign was mounted in the centre of a big tunnel wall, the text was black, embossed on a white metro brick tiled background, fixed solidly at eye level. A red arrow located close to the station sign pointed right where an exit from the platform led to concrete steps which went upwards. Donald followed the route and leisurely tracked the designated course by following further red arrows. As he approached the top level, he was surprised to see that he was now standing in a central part of the Riverside transport museum. An area he knew as 'Replica Street'. A street created to look like a Glasgow street of the Victorian era, but it was more akin to a movie set than an actual road. He couldn't see any red arrows pointing the way to Nostalgia, or a shop front fascia hinting tell-tale signs that this mysterious venue was close by or if it existed or not. It was as if he was a child again, having the whole museum to himself, an adult playground.

In the meantime, as he waited for Nostalgia to appear, or someone to invite him in, he decided to observe Replica Street.

The first time Donald set eyes on the place was a few weeks after the Riverside museum opened in 2011. Back then, he felt as though he transported to a film set of old Glasgow. This time was different and much better.

Moving around the mock street, he saw many shops of different trades – a photographer's shop, a cabinet maker, a dressmaker, a sailmaker, cobblers, a café and a pub called Mitre. Old vintage trucks, cars, a tram and a horse-drawn hearse, which made him squirm slightly, were dotted around the museum. It was if the time of the ages went flying by and had emerged from the depths of the near-by Clyde to present a living memory to future visitors that this is how Glasgow once looked, or maybe not! He knew too well that the copy street looked nothing like an older Glasgow he had seen in magazines or books. The streets where children played in dirt and grime wearing shabby clothes, and were lucky to have footwear. But that's rose-tinted glasses for you. The olden days were the best, even though they weren't, in fact, they were far from it.

Suddenly, his attention is drawn to a sound of music emanating from somewhere behind the backlot – the temporary set construction as he saw it. He knew the sound, his dad played this song regularly on his HMV record player. The fuzz guitar followed by the pulsating bass, then drums followed the melody that proved to Donald that this was one of his dad's favourites.

Spirit in the sky soon filled the museum loudly, which made him think that the police may turn up soon, and he will in the back of the van with flashing lights. How could he answer their questions? "I was on the subway train looking for a place called Nostalgia." *Yeah, and I am sure a doctor would arrive. One wearing a white jacket and a sizeable hypodermic needle in one hand with the other forcing me to wear a straight-jacket. Take this man away, he is insane!*

He spent more time looking in every shop window in Replica Street. Window shopping of sorts. Something he very rarely did in Glasgow.

Donald stopped in his tracks. His vision drawn to The Mitre Pub, which now showed a new sign above the door. Nostalgia glared at him. The windows covered with frosted glass and lights were warm and glowing inside. As he walked towards the building, he placed an ear to the window, hoping to hear, or ascertain movement, or catch voices from inside.

At the door of this establishment, a small hatch was visible, just like in the movies, a speakeasy trap. Donald moved near to the door.

Three fistful knocks tapped the wooden door as he waited for a response. Almost immediately, the flap slid open and a face or an outsized moustache face came into view. *That damn inspector again,* he imagined.

"How can I help you, sir?" the doorman's voice erupted.

Before answering, Donald was unsure why this circus of events took him away from the course he had been recently lived. It all seems very theatrical and couldn't fathom out any bit of it. But he was there and carried on with the game. If it was one, it was just so hard to tell!

Donald held up the invite. "I have this ticket," he said pushing it in through the flap where a hand grasped the card, withdrew hastily inside and the flap closed firmly.

Charming, he thought.

A few quiet moments past. Donald stared patiently at the door flap waiting for a response.

Several bolts were heard unlocking when the oversized red door flew open, the same small man, the conductor, this time dressed as a barman, appeared before Donald. His attire now included a white shirt, featuring attached red pinstriped two-button waistcoat, a black bow tie and black arm garters with a white waist apron. His hair was waxed and parted in the middle. He had an enormous walrus moustache which covered his mouth. The same man again. The owner, or general manager of Nostalgia. Whoever he was, he invited Donald inside.

"Welcome to Nostalgia, sir, please take a seat, and I will pour you Grahamston's finest Alston stout. A brew like Alston's will make you lick your whiskers, that's for sure."

"What whiskers?" he whispered to himself.

A phrase he must have used on many occasions, he guessed. If others had made a similar trip? The same old worked routine for every guest that visits Nostalgia.

Still, no mouth or teeth visible, but a rosy chin shone like a beacon sitting static under the most prominent moustache ever seen. His mouth was speaking, but his face gave no moveable signs of this action. A ventriloquist dummy has more facial movements, he believed.

Donald spent the next few moments staring at the incredible beauty of the place he entered.

Nostalgia was huge. Every part of the room was more significant in scale than that of the Mitre Inn he remembered that sat on Replica Street. Like the Beachcomber bar at Butlin's, he reminded himself when on holiday as a boy, it was a Beachcomber bar but felt different. It had a sizeable shipwrecked boat as a centrepiece which sat in a clear pool of water, fishermen's nets and ropes hung from the old boat wreck which dangled into the water below, more net's and lobster pots swung precariously low from the ceiling with oil lanterns wavering on chains which dimly lit the place. Towering palm trees scattered everywhere, bamboo seating and tables sat in between further display items. The bar, where the moustache man stood preparing Donald's drink, looked as though it could have been the film set of *Swiss Family Robinson*. Plastic, display model seagulls were suspended by nylon, and a few toy parrots of many different colours sat perched on the bar top. For a finale, a partition surrounding, a humongous photographic image of a Polynesian beach covered the entire wall completely. As if he was standing on a deserted island. He felt like a petulant pirate or maybe Robinson Crusoe, the hero of his childhood.

He took a seat, still looking around the Beachcomber bar, and seeing objects he missed on his first glance. A pirate's chest, a waterfall with white cascading foamed water which was illuminated with an intense yellow underwater light. The place looked dream-like but enjoyable to his well-being.

His fantasy trance broke when two large glasses of Alston Stout were placed forcibly on the table before him. "Enjoy your beer, sir," said the barman as he briskly strode back towards the bar.

Donald's hand took a grip on the handle, but the weight of the ale took him by surprise. He raised the massive glass tanker with slight difficulty. The goblet overflowed with a thick brown beer with a creamy beige head. He supped inquisitively, expecting a horrible aftertaste, but was surprised at the soft palate and coffee tasting beer he swallowed. He took a further large gulp or two before placing the tumbler on the table. A wipe with the back of his hand did more than enough to remove any remnant of beer foam that surrounded his lips.

"Are you going to drink both beers?" said a man's voice approaching Donald from his rear.

Another heartfelt moment that made his whole frame shudder. Shaking uncontrollably, he ventured to leave the comfort of his seat to stand.

A hand swayed forwards which Donald accepted and shook passionately.

"Are you?" he stammered. He was scared and wary, and very unsure of the situation.

"Yes. I'm your dad. But I see very clearly that you are much older than I am."

Although standing close together, Donald gave a thousand-yard stare to the man he knew as his father. The man in the family photographs. A man from 1970, and the man he remembered from his childhood. It was his dad!

Pulling Donald's arm towards him, he gave the best bear hug Donald ever had. A tight and genuine dad-hug which he always wanted and had dreamt of.

"You're my dad! I can't believe this, you are my dad!"

Both hugged each other for a very long time. A time that was lost long ago but not forgotten. Donald was a little boy again.

James Forbes was 28 when he died. His life, sadly taken almost immediately when a speeding driver struck him on a busy road near his home. The hit and run driver, although seen by several witnesses, was never traced, though a few late-night stragglers that witnessed the horrific crime gave a good description of the grey saloon car but could not identify the driver, or his passenger.

Donald was still wool-gathering as he listened without offering any questions, he just willingly heard his dad rambling on about memories, all which he loved as the smile on his face proved. He was now spending time with his dad as the young Donald always wished.

Beer kept landing on the table, one after the other, and all large tumblers filled foaming with Alston stout which grew in taste with every gulp.

James was still the 28-year-old man that appeared before Donald – dressed in 1970 apparel. Donald recollected men's fashions from that decade where he saw shocking mustard knits, dazzling patterns, high waists, way-too-skimpy briefs, flares and suede chukka boots and other fashion faux pas that defy description for the mind-set of the present-day gentleman.

"Can I ask you a question, Dad?" Donald said easily.

"Of course. If I know the answer, I will tell you the truth."

"Where am I now?" was his first offering, which although not the question James thought would be asked, it was a question and poignant.

"You are in Nostalgia. It's a meeting place for souls."

"Am I dead?"

"Not at all. A sepheric sanctuary like this place is a place where the dead are not dead and the living not alive. Anything more than that I cannot give answers. I'm sorry."

"Am I here because of what I said in the classroom in 1970?"

"Partly. But there is so much more. Turn around and look at the screen," James solemnly said as both stared at a white screen that had materialised close-by. The screen flickered, it was the start of an old super-8 cine film. A film showed a wedding from a long time ago. The marriage of Donald's parents at the Dennistoun New Parish Church in 1961 which he immediately recognised. Flamboyant fashion, which included straight-legged suits and thin ties and an abundance of charcoal suits, from Slaters, he imagined. The older generation wore a more traditional dress. A splattering of kilts gave a Scottish feel, and women in attire of many colours and hats that suited the ages. Senior women wore dull looking pillbox hats and mid-aged woman had bow fascinators that matched their floral dresses. Younger women wore miniskirts with gaudy wide brim hats as they all looked as though they would steal the show, apart from the bride, that is!

Guests were entering the church, and smiling faces were everywhere in view. They are turning their bright faces towards the super-8 cine camera. The older generation stood still and expected a photograph, they didn't know they were extras in a Glasgow movie. Sullen looks emanated from the grumpy faces that this old generation seemed to divulge to the youth of 1961. An out of focus close-up of the minister delivering his ceremony, and a shot of James putting the ring on the bride's finger. Then the bride is kissing the groom. The film jumped slightly, and a few burn marks appeared on the screen before guests were shown leaving the church to the sound of a lone piper, though hearing the bagpipes was a different matter. It was a silent movie after all.

Confetti, haphazardly thrown with enthusiasm over the bride and groom as they attempted shelter by bowing as low as they could, which did no good whatsoever. Multiple family and friends jumped into a group to take photographs, though the paid professional organised the choreography to capture that unique moment that would give a lifetime of joy.

Family photographs would later prove and show, handfuls of Polaroid's of decapitated people, faces of guests intruding on the perfect shot, drunk poses and general pictures of the wedding cake.

Mockingly, the best man's speech was always a good picture to capture. The first dance of the bride and groom created a stir amongst the party, the band under the coloured lights, depending on the consumption of drinks, or if any good film remained in the camera.

Suddenly, the frame showed a sign that filled most of the screen.

Welcome to Butlin's Ayr!

Soon, old flickering amateur film footage appeared on the screen. A clear image of the child Donald jumping on a trampoline with a few Redcoat supervisors in attendance and a close-up view of baby John Forbes in his buggy crying. His mum is smiling close to the lens. Dad playing crazy golf and acting silly, a scary large man on stilts that none of the children liked and ballroom dancing with many couples swirling around the room. A couple floated over the floor with no care in the world. A happier looking pair, if there ever was one. Professional in approach to dancing, but purely amateur in style of grace.

The swimming pool looked busy today, and Donald was seen splashing his mum with handfuls of cold pool water. The dancing couple also sat near the Forbes family enjoying the fun and frolics. *Were they friends?* entered Donald's mind.

The next view showed a beautiful sunny day: the children ate and drank sugar products. Donald showed a chocolate grin with a few teeth absent from his satisfied smile. Three families enjoyed the space they allocated themselves. It looked like a picnic area was set on a grassy clearing near the beach. Setting up a few deck chairs, a windbreak and two tartan rugs to hold the picnic assortment of goodies. They ate cold sandwiches served on paper plates, possibly egg with salad cream, chicken, spam and brown sauce, tuna and cucumber, cheese and tomato, boiled ham and pickle with mixed bags of potato crisps. Cheese and onion, the favoured choice. People were drinking tea and coffee poured from tartan covered vacuum flasks. Happy faces all waving towards the camera.

The ageing film showed Donald's dad playing football on the beach with other eager adults when the game was suddenly interrupted by a frantic scene of hysterical screaming women running towards the ocean. The camera followed the running crowd. The extract changed as if a documentary was in full production – the film kept rolling, and the camera direction rotated towards the incoming sea that was throwing its weight onto the sand 100 yards or more in the distance. The lens refocused on the situation developing, and the filmmaker walked steadily towards the developing action where a large group had now assembled. Men were discarding clothes and stripping off to their underwear before hastily diving into the cold water of the firth of Clyde that covered the expanse of the Ayrshire coast. Someone must be in difficulty in the water. There must have been ten men, or more, in the sea, all swimming as fast as their diverse talent could take them. Two men in a rowing boat were in the water close by the action. All are heading in one direction. All trying to reach a small boy in difficulties many yards from the safety of the beach. Now focussed and filming the scene as it happened, the film stopped – no more film in the camera. The screen turned blank, then white, followed by red burn blisters that covered the screen, then the movie stopped.

"I can't remember seeing this film," Donald said calmly. "What happened?" he added.

"This is the first time I have seen it also," spoke James. "But it is as I remember," said, James.

"Who was the young boy drowning and was he saved?"

"He was saved. And, thankfully, I was the strongest swimmer, and managed to reach the boy and return him to the safety of the beach. I gave mouth-to-mouth resuscitation which brought him back to life, he was dead for over a minute. A doctor and an ambulance crew arrived soon after and acknowledged me for my efforts. All of which, if I hadn't got to him when I did, he would not have survived. So, they said."

Donald stared at the blank cine screen.

"Who was the boy?"

"He was a young boy from Glasgow. Ian Shaw was his name. His parents were so thankful that I saved his life, even though I never sought glory for my effort.

"His mother approached me once the boy was alive and well. She said, without me acting so courageously and swiftly, she could no longer be a mother.

"'I could have lost my only child,' she repeated."

Donald stood still and did not waver or stumble even after many full beers he had consumed. He turned to face his father.

"I know Ian Shaw. I met him recently in Glasgow. Ian Shaw is a police officer."

"He was also the young man that saved the life of the baby girl that fell from a tenement window," said Donald's dad interrupting politely. "I know Ian Shaw was the young man that jumped into the Clyde attempting to save your life when you made a brave attempt to save another.

"Do you remember any of this?" he added.

"Yes, he is also the police officer that nearly crashed into the back of my taxi, I should have guessed there was further madness to this strange story, and I'm sure there is more to come," he said as he slumped onto the chair which enclosed his empty frame.

"What is all of this about? Is there a good ending to this story?"

Words were leaving his mouth, which he used as a tool to search for truth, a truth that would give a full clearer picture. As it stood, he thought there was no defined logic to any of this. It seems his mind offered no solace to the structure of this odd dream that had followed him invariably. *Will this ever end? Will normality return to my life?* He provided himself with these thoughts over and over.

"Donald, you are here for a special reason. A reason that will help a pure soul work tirelessly for others. A heart that will create more love in a world that constantly needs love. And importantly, uncontaminated from evil. A love that is as bright as a star."

"I don't understand any of this. My mind can't cope with all this information churning through my head. I cannot comprehend any of this, I'm sorry," said Donald, surrendering his feelings.

"There is someone special that wants to meet with you, Donald," said his dad. Turning his head gently, Donald saw a strange man approach, he held an outstretched hand towards Donald who instinctively accepted and shook firmly.

Donald just stood beside his seat staring at the man before him. A man he somehow knew. As they stared intently into each other's eyes, Donald felt a bond simmer within him. He felt charged as a battery would when a weird surge of energy rushed through every part of his body. A warm glow bubbled within his inner conscience that allowed information that had lain dormant, re-emerge and focus to the front of his thoughts. A reboot of his soul was his thought as his ignorance could not fathom any of this. A few seconds more and Donald spoke his first word to the unfamiliar person.

"Dad!"

Both men threw outstretched arms around each other and held a tight embrace that lasted over a minute. The stranger moved backwards while gripping each shoulder of Donald.

"It's so good to meet my son again," the stranger spoke with a blessed voice.

A smile grew on the face of Donald as he moved forwards to grip the stranger once more tightly.

"Dad, we are together again," his voice gave way to his mind as his memory jumped forwards to his real dad, James, who sat close by him. He tried to deny any logic that was present and reacted.

"How can you be my dad? My dad is sitting here," pointing his finger towards James Forbes.

"We both are, Donald. We are your fathers. And you will find all this surreal and confusing. But it is with our best intentions that you are here today, here to listen to what we have to explain in detail why you are here in Nostalgia," said James Forbes, now standing near Donald.

"You are both my fathers. I have memories of you both," he spoke disbelievingly.

"My head is cluttered with information. So much knowledge that I really can't cope with it all."

"We are both fathers of you, Donald, and many, many more fathers have passed your many lives over other millennia. James is your current father, and I was your father previously. In a former life," the stranger offered.

"Do you mean reincarnation?" said Donald looking perplexed and anxious.

"Yes," said James

"But why, why am I here and meeting you both now?"

"Donald," said the stranger. "In your previous life, when I was your father. You know most of the story by now." He paused ever so slightly.

"You were Tommy Shaw. The boy that drowned so horrifically in the Clyde. My beloved young son Tommy."

Donald's nodding head showed a possibility that he began to understand that all of this may be true.

"Somehow, I seem to know this," Donald sat again. He continued with his questions.

"I know all of this. My mind has let me accept these facts as truth. It is bewildering, I must say. But I feel the truth."

"They are all true, Donald," said James Forbes taking Donald's hand to comfort him.

"So all the strange weirdness that has been happening to me is for me to help with something that happened in my previous life?" he said curiously.

"This life and your previous experience. We need your help to find a small wooden cross. A cross made from the wood of an olive tree that grew in the ancient soil within the garden of Gethsemane. A tree that Jesus himself ate the fresh and ripe olives," James said and continued, "A knight returned from the holy land and entrusted the relic to a family. Not a family of wealth or notoriety, but a good family that would help others less fortunate than themselves."

"Can't angels find the cross?" Donald enquired.

"Only a family member can source the cross and retrieve it, Donald. The power within the relic is divinely blessed, and only a living relative can give the cross to some other person linked to the family tree. Someone pure, just and incorruptible."

"So my memory may still know where I lost this cross, or where I put it or possibly hid it. And even more weird to say, obviously, when I was Tommy."

"Yes," both men said together.

"I feel as if I know where the cross is. I see images in my head as clear as day," Donald spoke as he looked towards both dads. "I know where I put it but don't know if it will still be there. Not now. So many years have since past."

He continued with newfound memories from his previous life. Nostalgia was giving Donald clear thoughts of his past life, and with an intake of fresh air, he spoke again.

"Me and my pals used to visit the Pots and Pans regular to see the weird curiosities. Also known as the Britannia Panopticon," he said with a wry smirk on his face. "We loved the Pots and Pans, it was always an experience. We would visit Madame Zita. An automated fortune-telling machine. A Gypsy woman predicted your future for a penny. But every time we played, we got bad cards. Never a good future came to any of us. Every card we received was either dull or boring, or sometimes scarily sad. One day, a worker was cleaning the machine and checking the movements. We watched as Madame Zita's moved left then right, then up and down, her automated hands moved over a row of playing cards as they normally did and showed her chest movement like she was breathing and she, of course, delivers a fortune card which the machine did several times during the maintenance check. The worker at one point left the glass case open as he nipped off for some tools or a tea break, and I jumped at the chance to slip the cross from my neck and attach it around her wax neckline and hid it under her lace blouse. I thought that this might change her predictions, hopefully, give better future readings," he said fully informed on his past life. He continued, "As soon as the machine was operational again, we checked our fortunes. Every card that came out of Madame Zita's machine was perfect. All the cards were encouraging, and gave hope and love quotations constantly, which in turn, gave everyone that used the machine a feeling of money well spent. People queued to use Madams Zita's fortune telling. It became the highlight for all that visited the Panopticon from that day onwards."

James Forbes was the first to react to his son's recollections.

"You must take the train to the Panopticon, Donald. Go now and find the cross."

Before Donald answered, he found himself back on the mock subway train, and it was moving fast. Once again, the make-believe stations appeared and disappeared as the train hurtled its way through the dark tunnels. Expecting this, among other weird anomalies he fully knew would happen, he sat waiting for his destination to arrive. Wherever this may be?

The train seemed to move forwards minute after minute, mile after mile, relentlessly taking Donald headlong to an unknown terminus. He spoke aloud to himself, "What do I do with the cross? If I find it?"

Instantly, the train stopped and appeared at an unknown station – one that Donald never knew existed. A large sign secured to cold white Metro tiles filled most of the wall. 'Brunswick Lane', a place he knew well and lay close to the Panopticon Theatre on the Trongate. The doors swished open, and he ventured out and took soft unsure steps onto the platform. Large posters promoting the Panopticon Theatre of weird and mysterious pleasures plastered every surrounding wall. The train vanished without noise and left him standing in a station that was pure make-believe. He was alone!

There was one set of steps leading upward which he took. Walking at a slow space, admiring and looking at more publicity posters that decorated the walls. Seeing one, in particular, that caught his eye. Madame Zita, the world's favourite fortune teller, faced him as he reached the top flight. Almost immediately, his attention was drawn to an old set of theatre doors. He attempted to open the rusty, corroded handles, but this didn't work. Shaking the doors gave no release. It was then he noticed a giant wall fixed bell sat protruding at the side of the entrance with a small sign saying: 'Please press'.

"As this mystery goes on, let's push the button," he said aloud.

Ring, ring, ring, rang loudly and the chimes sounded distant.

The noise was remote and remained lurid, by pressing the button again, the same echoed sound rang noisily. Suddenly, the doors swung open forcing Donald backwards and made him address his footing to stabilise his balance. Still unsure of what was ahead, he walked into the dimly lit passageway. The Panopticon, he guessed. As he moved towards the end of the walkway, a door appeared before him – a regular glazed door made of red-varnished wood with a glass frame at the top half. Black writing promoted the name: 'A E Pickard Theatrical Impresario', and a low desk light shone throw the glass. Although still participating in weird fantasy, he took time to knock on the door to which there was no reply. He managed to hit the glass frame once again and stood in anticipation as a mail carrier would do – wait for a response.

"Come in, Donald," a voice came forcibly through to reach Donald's ears which made him set his head back as if he never expected anyone to reply let alone mention him by name.

Donald turned the door handle slowly, it swung open to show a room what he would imagine being a Victorian office. His eyes adjusted to the dim light, and there before him, standing in front of an oak desk, stood a gentleman. This gentleman was in his late 50s, wearing a grey woollen three-piece suit, double-pleated and high-waisted trousers that sat proudly over a pair of low heel semi-brogue spectator shoes. This man was well turned out and looked every part a man of means. A gold pair of nose-pinched glasses sat at the end of his red bulbous nose and a large, well-trimmed, greying handlebar moustache sat neatly below. An intense bouquet of a fresh smelling gentleman's cologne filled the room, and a large bottle of the aroma sat proudly on the desk showing Donald that the gentleman was the purveyor of a luxury scent, a scent which he had never heard of, a fragrance called Fougère Royale by Houbigant. A delightful and beautiful aroma that would cost lots of money for such an expensive and lovely item as this, he imagined.

"Please come in, Donald," the gentleman offered.

Donald offered a question to the highly dressed man.

"How do you know my name and are you who I think you are?"

"I am A E Pickard. And you are Donald Forbes. I have been expecting you for a few days now."

"How did you know that I was coming here?" Donald wanted to ask many more questions.

A E Pickard was more than a showman, he felt now that he was part of a bigger show, even though there was no reason to understand the legitimacy of his involvement, the fact he was involved in a mystery beyond fiction itself, his participation was entirely accepted.

He told his story.

"It all happened over six months ago. There were huge queues of people waiting just for an opportunity to have their fortune read, which no one in Panopticon or me personally, could understand why this automated machine became suddenly famous. Everyone that used the device received advice and information they asked or prayed for.

"I ultimately stopped putting cards in the machine, yet it still gave out fortune cards. It was a miracle. And for me, this was a money-making opening if there ever was one. Can you imagine the opportunities that arose from owning such a machine? I could not contain the amount of money the device held. It became an overnight sensation. It attracted thousands of romantics to my theatre. Over the first few months, people were coming from all over to have a machine read their future, and I can tell you other businesspeople and showmen alike offered me unbelievable amounts of money for my prize asset. The press was continually at my door looking for comments and any exclusive information on the mysterious machine.

"But then, as the word spread further afield about its fame, I had every crook and criminal crawling from the woodwork trying to steal her. I had to pay for armed guards to stand and protect the machine every day of the week.

"Then one day, a day I will never forget, I heard a tapping noise emanating from my window, which I opened, yet I saw no one. This mystery happened irritatingly over an hour or so. Tap, tap, tap! Then the next time I looked, there was a crow perched on the window ledge and was tapping the window constantly. It was a strange and bizarre moment, especially for me, a showman extraordinaire of oddities and peculiarities, but this was so out of tune with any other eccentricities I had witnessed over my time in this business."

Pickard held a crystal decanter filled with whisky, poured two large glasses, and the gentleman handed one tumbler to Donald which he accepted, as Pickard thought that this would do ample justice to the occasion. For both men.

The gentleman perched himself on the edge of his desk a few feet from Donald.

He took a large gulp of whisky and Donald followed suit.

"I opened the window, and the crow didn't attempt to fly off or make any further noise. It flew into my office. Then, without a word of a lie." He paused as if gathering thoughts. "The crow transformed into a man. A tall, lean olive-skinned man with black wavy hair and stood over 6 ft in height, dressed in black and wearing a long black knee-length coat."

He swallowed another glass of whisky.

"I'm a simple man, Donald, with modest hopes and aspirations for my life. Business is different, of course, but here I was stuck in a situation I would never have dreamt of ever being subject to – a day when everything changed. I listened intently and would agree to all the requests the olive man asked. He had told me that he was a guardian sent from the holy land.

"I felt the goodness emanating from him, I felt my body react oddly, but not wrong or in an evil way. I was comfortable and willing only to listen and help in any way I could. He told me that you would arrive someday soon. Donald Forbes, from the future, and that you would want to see Madame Zita. I never asked why. All of this was well out of my field of conscious – way beyond my limited brain power, my beliefs or any suitable reason I held.

"Anyway, we chatted, and I was to act. I was on a quest!

"My first job was to inform the press that I had sold Madame Zita to a showman from New Jersey. Apologise to my customers for losing this most popular automated machine but, as a businessman, the offer was seemingly far too good to refuse. I organised a large wooden chest to be loaded onto a truck outside the theatre and to let the public see this removal take place. The daily papers said I had sold Madame Zita to a businessman in New York. Thankfully, the newspapers printed a fabricated story of Madam Zita heading for America."

A E Pickard walked from his desk towards a large solid looking cabinet, took a key from his waistcoat pocket and opened the dresser.

"This is the reason you are here, Donald."

"Wow!" was the only word that left Donald's mouth. Followed soon by others. "Madame Zita, how on earth."

"Yes, I was to keep it safe and away from prying eyes and from the hands of thieves."

Donald walked towards the machine and seemed fascinated with the look of the automated Madame Zita.

"Here is a penny, Donald. Ask her a question," said the gentleman handing over a gleaming penny.

Donald gently inserted the penny and turned a large brass handle. With music playing from deep inside the machine, Madame Zita nodded her head, bent her body sideways and her green glass eyes stared into Donald's. Her right hand moved left towards a card which she grabbed, she pulled solidly on the card which she then ran over an open chute and dropped the printed voucher to an expectant Donald.

Picking the card from the open drop box, he placed it into his jacket pocket without observing the reading.

"Can I ask what day this is? Or what year it is?" Donald forced out two quick questions.

The gentleman walked around behind his desk and opened the red velvet curtains that hung over a large window to show Donald a night full of heavy snow and low-lit gas street lamps that gave a warm appeal to a cold view and people rushing, as all Xmas shoppers do. Horses-pulled carts, some wagons had been abandoned, and hackney cabs sluggishly moved through the slushy snow.

"It's Christmas Eve 1932, Donald. Just in time for the festivities." Donald looked strangely at the gentleman as he waited for A E Pickard to give him information about past events.

"Just this morning, a small boy came to my office. He wore metal callipers on each leg. A sickly-looking boy if I ever saw one. He told me a story, a story that the olive man had previously mentioned."

More whisky was poured and consumed.

"The boy knew a young girl, a girl of 16, and she had fallen pregnant and gave birth to a baby girl. He called the baby, Jeanie. Anyway, the mother was homeless and living in appalling conditions under a railway arch near Central Station. She was in feeble health, and the baby was not being fed or clothed sufficiently. A very dire circumstance indeed."

Pickard filled both glasses with a fill of whisky which he gulped half.

"I was to provide room and board for both the girl and her baby, give protection and a haven, and more importantly – prepare her for a journey. I was informed that the girl was to be taken back to her time. She arrived from the future, Mr Forbes, and the future she was to return. Evil was searching for her, and I was to protect her until she moved home.

"There is more to this life than I could ever imagine. Stranger than any dream or nightmare I have ever had, or story I could possibly write." AE Pickard finished the remaining whisky then laid the glass on his desk. "The girl and her baby left today on the Balmanno Express to a future that I am sure you will have knowledge. But you are here for another reason?" Pickard walked to the machine of Madame Zita, and opened a glass door which gave entrance to the internal workings and access to the automated puppet. He stood back as Donald approached.

Donald placed both hands around the neck of Madame Zita, and by exploring under the lace collar that sat entirely above her shoulders, he searched and immediately found what he had come for. A small wooden cross held on a gold chain which he removed, as if by magic, from the neck of the puppet. He held it as to offer A E Pickard a glimpse of the artefact before inserting it into an inside jacket pocket.

"You have a train to catch, Donald," was the only words offered before Donald found himself back sitting on the Balmanno Express which was moving fast. He sat alone and stared curiously at the intricate cross that lay in the palm of his hand as warm energy pulsated through his tired body which invigorated his spirit. A smile appeared over his face, and warm tears dripped from his eyes onto the small cross. Music now played on the train. Donald had knowledge of the song, though never heard, he understood the sweet and beautiful song was, *Servant to the slaves*, by the Scottish band, Capercaillie. A song that would not be released until 1991 was further information gathered on this paranormal journey.

The song played from beginning to end as Donald sat in silence and wondered where his next mystery would lead.

Crowning Glory

The curious and thought-provoking inquisitive story of the mysterious visitor to Tommy Shaw's grave had become entrenched in local folklore, and the enigma sprouted wings as the years passed. A carefree myth that graveyard workers encouraged others to perpetuate that the legend of the mystery grave guest was none other than an angel or a divine spirit. However, another unearthly story remained connected with Tommy's grave, beer hall whispered rumours flourished that a crow would sit perched on the cold marble gravestone for hours on end and cry some bird song. The urban fable further stated that this crow would arrive on Tommy's birthday and stay all day, even if scared off, the bird would tirelessly return and only leave after the sun went down. These annual events created an everlasting, time-gripping fable that would carry forever forwards and hold a unique bond to the untimely death of the unfortunate small boy, Tommy Shaw.

Many years past since the remains of the missing boy, the boy from the River Clyde, young Tommy Shaw had been discovered then buried alongside both his parents, the yearly burial ground visitor always, without failure, laid a sprig of heather and left a few lines of poetry on his final resting place.

In the worker's hut, that sits unstable near the entrance to the cemetery, collected poems are taken from the graveside and held as evidence to prove the mysterious mourner is factual and not fictitious. The worker's pride and joy was the latest oddity to arrive at the weird, and an entirely oddball collection of nautical rhymes added healthy inquisitiveness to the folklore.

A Robert Louis Stevenson poem called *Requiem*.

Under the wide and starry sky
Dig the grave and let me lie.
Glad did I live and gladly die,
And I laid me down with a will.
This be the verse you grave for me;
'Here he lies where he longed to be,
Home is the sailor, home from sea,
And the hunter home from the hill'.

No identifying note of the evasive visitor was ever left or found. It remained a bewildering story full of intrigue. The Shadow Angel, a local newspaper epithet for the undiscovered fellow of the night, was a regularly used metaphor for any strange occurrence that had no proof of identity or if you wanted to scare someone; use the name; Shadow angel!

But, however vigilant the locals were to identify this elusive character, the tradition would remain anonymous and mysterious, and the force of human frailty would once again shake and shape the story every way possible to suit every occasion.

Party to Party

It was Sunday, the 25th of March, 2001. Donald found himself sitting silently in his stationary taxi, and the smirk on his face promoted a wide grin as his image glared back to him from the interior mirror. The sun was shining bright, and the day was lovely. Donald found himself pondering his next move, and what would this current journey offer, but before any decision was made or attempting to discover where he found himself or what time in history procrastination delivered him, the driver's door opened.

"Donald, good to see you again. I have been expecting you. Come, the party is about to begin!" said Jessie Brook enthusiastically.

Without conversation, or doubting his sanity, he knew exactly where he was, he followed Jessie to her house.

A group of around twenty people filled the elegant small lounge, and beyond open patio doors to the rear of the room, a few more guests were in conversation as they socially circulated, on the paved stone patio, in a beautifully tendered garden. Donald was introduced to most of the guests and had a glass of bubbly forcibly put in his hand as Jessie Brook called those in attendance to order. A champagne flute was hit several times with a small teaspoon which suddenly brought the chitchat to a halt.

"Everyone, I would like to thank you for attending Violet's birthday today, and not just any birthday. Its Violet's coming of age party, the big 21st!"

Everyone cheered.

"Please join me in song," she added as the guests were led by Jessie singing, *Happy birthday*, loud and clear.

Violet danced among the gathering, thanking each one, she smiled and laughed and looked forever happy. Now visibly joyful, she saw Donald standing covertly to the rear of the party, though he swiftly managed to slip into the garden to find a quieter spot away from the melee of youth.

"Donald, I'd like to introduce you to a dear friend of ours, Jonathon Dailly," offered Jessie as Donald took his hand and shook it firmly.

"It's good to meet you at last, Donald. I've heard so much about you!" offered the gentleman.

Donald had a visible strange mystified look over his face. His judgements were scrambled enough that no conclusion could be reached, nor could he offer a response, he was bemused. Unexpectedly, a cheerful Violet appeared to join the small cluster that had moved onto the lawn.

"Good to see you, Donald, and I thank you for coming to my party," said the sweet innocent voice of Violet.

Donald was swift to respond, and before he could ascertain his move, his body and mind worked in tandem.

"I have a present for you, Violet. I just hope you like it," he said removing an envelope from his pocket.

"Thank you, Donald. Thank you so much. There was no need."

Violet spoke as the envelope was opened to show a typical 21st birthday card. But what was different to this card was the fact that an object was sellotaped to the inside portion. A gold chain with a small wooden cross which dangled freely and made Violet gasp for air.

"It's beautiful, Donald!" Violet kindly responded.

She kissed and hugged Donald responsively and offered more grateful and compassionate words of thanks.

"Let me do the honour, young lady," said Jonathon Dailly as he took the chain and wrapped it carefully around the slender neck of Violet and attached the pinch bail with ease, as the cross hung on her chest.

"It's so beautiful, Donald. I cannot thank you enough."

Her pride glowed, she was impulsive to show her friends this unique and beautiful gift. A gift she did not know the full history or effect it would have over her future life or well-being.

The party continued onwards as the darkness began to seep in on the bright day that had seen much fun and laughter.

"Are you heading back to Glasgow, Donald?" said Jonathan Dailly as he caught hold of Donald's arm as he made his way back to the house.

Just before Donald could offer any response, he found himself back in his taxi, parked at the front of a very long row of cabs, all patiently waiting for customers to arrive.

And without any knowledge or discussion from his passenger, he knew he was back in the present day. He looked older again. His passenger, he could see clearly in the rear-view mirror, was Jonathon Dailly.

His taxi was parked on West George Street, just a few yards from the lively George Square. It was Christmas Eve, and he had a party to attend this evening. A party he did not want to miss.

Donald turned to see the well-dressed man sitting comfortably in the centre of the seat. He looked very much like the man he met at the party. An elderly gent and probably near his own age.

"Can you take me to Stan's studio cafe on Alexander Park Street, please?" said Jonathon Dailly.

"I know the cafe, Mr Dailly. It's just a short journey," Donald said as he started the engine and drove forwards, as the gentleman sat silently, hoping to enjoy the quick drive.

The travel time was brief, and no more words passed between either man, that is until they stopped close by the cafe.

"Do you have some time to listen to a story, Donald?"

Donald's mystified look was less than he expected, but something he knew was appropriate with his beautiful life these days. Another time when all oddities seem weird and all that isn't, probably was.

"You know my name? And how do you know my name?" he was facing the back of his taxi but still strapped in with the tight seat belt.

"My name is Jonathon Dailly."

Donald's stare covered every inch of his passenger's body but gave careful added attention to his face. Both men stared intently into each other's eyes.

"I knew you. Are you, are you the same Jonathon Dailly that I tried to save from the Clyde many years ago?" Donald offered as he unbuckled the seat belt that held him tightly in the seat. "You disappeared from the hospital."

"If you have time to spare for 30 minutes or so, and a quick coffee, I will gladly tell you my story," said Jonathon Dailly inquiringly.

The snack bar is a part cafe, and a slice of art studio fusion. Artwork adorns every wall with creative art from many local artists, with a simple yet straightforward look, and if it's true that we eat with our eyes, then this small eatery offers more than most. The menu shares an assortment of delicious cakes and coffee, or as someone made a precise comment on TripAdvisor and said, "I love coming here! It's such a sweet treat to the soul. If you are in Glasgow, PLEASE visit for coffee and nihilism."

Well, after all the baffling trips Donald had been on previously, maybe nihilism was short of the mark, especially in his case.

The black taxi parked close by the small cafe, and both Donald and his passenger walked a few short steps to the eatery.

As the door swung open, a greeting of a friendly voice came towards them when a soft, yet happy reception welcomed them.

"Good afternoon, gentlemen, please take a seat," said the girl pointing towards a window table where two wicker seats sat tucked close to the table top.

"My name is Sarah, and this is my studio café. If you would like to have a look at the menu, it would be my pleasure to serve you." The warm welcome greeted them.

"Sarah, I would just like a latte please, and you, Donald?" said Jonathon Dailly.

"Same for me please," Donald agreed.

"Very well, gentlemen, your coffee will be here shortly," said Sarah as she left to prepare the hot drinks.

The studio was quiet, it was Christmas Eve and late afternoon. A few people, probably regulars, sat dotted around the small eating area where food and drinks were served. Some customers stood and glanced at the impressive assemblage of artwork which adorned the walls that added a warm, pleasant feel to the place.

"We obviously travelled through time, and you must be an angel or Jesus. Because I have not met another person that has made this unknown type of journey, apart from myself," whispered Donald softly, knowing other people sat a few feet away and didn't want anyone to hear his fragmentary comment.

"I'm not Jesus, nor am I an angel. We came here today under the instruction of Jesus. You see, Donald, like you, I have Jesus in my life and both our lives have run a similar course, crossing many paths we have ventured, many notions that we could easily not recognise, but for the love of God, we find ourselves at a crossroad where we meet to share our divine allocated moments. That brief singularity in time, a time when a quirky, peculiar change enters our most mundane existence, to enhance the life of others. And I know too well that you have knowledge of particle intervention."

"Your latte, gentlemen. Please enjoy!" said the charming host, Sarah, as two large hot mugs were placed on the table.

Both thanked her.

Jonathon Dailly continued,

"We, among many more people, more than you could ever imagine, Donald, serve the greater good. Help in any way we can. In fact, assist in many weird and wonderful ways, always attempting to halt evil in its tracks and to provide a clear pathway for the righteous to walk. This is an ongoing fight that we must always win. Not surrender or retreat, but with faith, we must allow ourselves the gift of life to enhance our capabilities in the daily struggle that faces us."

Donald listened intently. He had questions but allowed Jonathon to continue,

"Back in 1987, when my life was low. I attempted to take my own life. Suicide is such a scary, taboo subject. I was blind to the real facts and could not see past the pain.

"It was a different substance for me, and I needed the pain to disappear, I needed to be left alone.

"I once had a good life, Donald.

"I was married with a small child, I had a good earning job, and everything was rosy in the garden. But one day, the most terrible day of my life. On the way to church, I was bundled forcibly into the back of a car, taken to an abandoned warehouse and injected with a concoction of drugs.

"That day changed my life.

"In an instant, I was an addict, I also took pills regularly, I became dependent on alcohol, I stole from my wife and child. Then, eventually, I lost my family and job. Later, I became homeless, and more importantly, I was afraid. Two evil men started and repeated this abuse to me, yet they offered me alcohol and drugs free. I was dependent on them more than anyone, including my family. I knew they were evil. They wanted to destroy me and defeat any work I was currently endeavouring. Just to break the chain of events.

"They had me in their grip. I never understood why I was chosen. Why me? I didn't know any previous life at that point. I was just a simple married man with a small child, working 40 hours a week like most of my friends and neighbours.

"Earlier that night, before we met on the bridge, they had beaten me badly, I just couldn't cope with any more violence and constant intimidation. No further trouble from either of them I prayed. I prayed aloud, and they laughed. 'Where is your feeble God?' they kept shouting.

"They encouraged me to take my own life. Even offering me a blade to slit my throat, they laughed when I attempted to do it, but I couldn't, which angered them more.

"They began standing on my face and kicked my ribs for what seemed an eternity, and as a last insult, they covered me with urine.

"I was a lost soul.

"My shoes, my old worn-out tattered shoes, were ripped from my feet. I had no more strength, I had nothing, not one possession to claim as mine. The only thing they could not take was my faith. My firm beliefs held me together over the few months of torture those evil perpetrators bestowed upon me. But the last day was enough. I needed a way out.

"It took so much strength to walk from the city centre to the bridge, especially with no shoes on my cold, numb feet, and the injuries my body suffered. But I managed it! I was alone and would leave alone. I accepted my fate gladly, and at last, I could lose the brutality, the pain, the depression, the incessant suffering, the constant hunger and all the problems that come with being homeless.

"People don't see a homeless person. We are invisible at night, we are ugly old beggars in daylight, some with mental issues, others with health problems, most with money concerns, many with no family to ask for help. Of course, there is alcohol and drugs abuse among our collection of streetwalkers that most people avoid, yet we are only hoping to survive. Homeless people are in a constant struggle with many aspects of life, Donald, not because of evil perpetrators, but because each passer-by who looks on, does nothing.

That is till I met you and Tommy Shaw."

"You know Tommy Shaw?" interrupted Donald.

"Let me explain. You gave me hope. I saw goodness in you, I knew a good man stood with me on the bridge and would try his utmost to save my life. And for that, I am genuinely grateful.

"I jumped into the Clyde when I was at the lowest point in my existence. No helpful feelings rushed through me once I hit the icy water, they were long gone. My soul was moving to a place I did not know, but where I was going, I felt no fear. Now ready to face my demons!

"The devil was there. In the water. Observing me drown. I didn't see him, but I knew he was watching. When you came to my rescue, I saw the police officer jump in the river, two men of a similar age to myself, risking their own precious lives for the sake of another, I felt guilty, but also pride – and a flicker of hope for the future of the human race after I was gone.

"But when you disappeared, I felt heartbroken. The good man, the lifesaver, has drowned and lost his precious life, due to my personal will of self-destruction. It was later I found out you were very much alive. Thank God!

"I lost consciousness, then I saw a light, a bright, brilliant light that I began to travel towards. Then, abruptly, I heard the voice of a boy singing,

Row, row, row your boat gently down the stream.
Merrily, merrily, merrily, merrily life is but a dream.

"I started to float back through the dark, cold water towards the surface – that is when I was raised onto the rescue boat.

"Later that night, as I lay in the hospital, I detected a tapping noise on the window. A tapping noise just as I listened to all those years ago when I was a boy lying sick in bed. Once again, it took much effort to make a move, I struggled in pain on the way to the window which I managed to prise open. My heart missed a beat! A black crow flew into the room and transformed into a man. I was scared but immediately realised, I felt warm and satisfied that this magic was determined to work for good and not evil. My soul was being charged with a beautiful spirit, and it was if I had died and gone to heaven.

"A few hours ahead, I was mysteriously removed from the hospital and found myself located in a room called Nostalgia.

"As soon as I set foot in Nostalgia, which looked like the interior of a medieval castle, I knew then I had been here before, in fact, I had been many times before. All memories of my previous lives surged through my veins like a raging river of knowledge that gave information which lay dormant within me. I am sure I had many lives before my first experience, but the one I recall most was what started my rebirth timeline, and when all of this was set in motion, way back in 1099.

"My name was Richard Comtois from Picardy in Northern France, and I was in service to the Lord Baldwin

Des Marets, and we were on Europe's 1st Crusade to the Holy Land. On the 7th of June 1099, we reached Jerusalem. Many of our crusaders wept openly at the site of the city as we approached, a town we fought so hard to achieve. It took eight hard-fought days to win control of the magnificent and ancient dwelling place.

"However, what I witnessed was the total annihilation of every human being imprisoned within the olden walls. A massacre of people of all religions, all ages. A genuinely original horror I had ever borne witness, as innocent blood flowed through every street we walked.

"After we controlled the stronghold, a few friends and I found somewhere peaceful to rest near the Kidron Valley at a place known as the Garden of Gethsemane, the place where Jesus prayed the night of his betrayal and where he sweat drops of blood. We were tired and hungry, and ate our first food in days. We were plied with olives, bread and fish, which did more than quench our appetites. I awoke early one morning to the sound of a crying baby, a baby that looked no older than a few days. The young woman that held him sang a moving, short poetic rhyme to her child and I was the only knight awake that heard this. As I got close to her, I distinctly listened to her words. French words that proved to me she had travelled as part of our army, but she was alone and in need of help. The baby cried, and the mother sang prophetic words, 'My baby Prodo do not cry, my only prayer is that you die, and new life becomes you in pastures new, with the light of love all over you.'

"The woman had no energy, no food for her baby. She did not want her young child to live in this world of extreme violence or religious hatred, she prayed his life would end and to find a future life where he could blossom and live in a better world. She placed a small object around the baby's neck, laid him on the soil next to her, and collapsed and died almost instantly. Before I could say words to God, a figure approached, this figure was blessed, I knew the man standing before me was Jesus. I sank to my knees and prayed for forgiveness for all my sins. I wept openly. His hand touched my head which sent a surge of energy through my body to overwhelm my senses which confirmed that I was in the company of the son of God.

"I was told to rise, and take the baby and raise him as my own son. Take him to the land of Scotland and the baby's destiny would increase. The boy was to be known as Shaul, a Hebrew boys name, which means asked for God!

"It took several years to reach Scotland, and the boy was four years old when we set foot on Scottish soil, his name was now Tamhas Richard Shaw, and this boy grew to be your forbearer and all your family connections from that day forwards came from this one man, Thomas Richard Shaw. You have this man's blood flowing through your veins."

Donald was enthralled by the man's story. He listened further.

"I have been many people through many lives. In fact, during one incarnation, we both met.

"Do you remember Albert Ernest Pickard?"

"You were Pickard?" Donald questioned immediately.

"Yes, I was AE Pickard. I knew when I first arrived in Scotland in 1904 and had recently purchased the Gaiety Theatre in Clydebank that I had more than a business to occupy me. Shortly after my move to Scotland, I knew I had work to do, not just theatre life, but work for a higher power. After a brief visit to Nostalgia, my life as Pickard, I soon realised, that there were more pressing issues to deal with, and my main concern was to introduce your grandparents William and Morganna. Initially, this was a responsibility that gave me many problems, but, thankfully, all connections worked out in the end.

"Sometimes, people like me work to help particle intervention, create a change for good, by assisting others in choosing the proper road to walk or the right action to undertake, and at the appropriate time, all factors matter. I offered an opening to your grandfather to appear on stage alongside the future Stan Laurel, an offer he willingly accepted, though he knew his life was not made for entertainment or treading the boards as Stanley's life would eventually lead. William's energy flowed through every wall in the Panopticon and his love for theatre was visible to all that worked there, especially to a young American dancer, your grandmother, Morganna Stone.

"Let's just say, it all worked out well in the end. But like any war, there are many battles to win. We are always ready to fight another day." Jonathon paused. His mind was in thought.

He continued,

"When I left Nostalgia back in 1987, just after I disappeared from my hospital bed, I found myself instantaneously walking through the main doors of Heathrow Airport, terminal 4, with one ticket for the First-Class flight to JFK, New York. A luggage trolley was being pulled along by my left hand which felt full, and it was, with an assortment of clothes and footwear. I was immaculately dressed in a tailored pin-striped Armani suit with a white shirt and coordinated silk tie. The shoes were beautiful Oxford brogues. The ticket prompted British Airways, and I walked to the desk in a full-blown air of confidence. It was as if I was a British Agent, on a mission to stop some overweight wealthy internationalist from creating havoc against the free world. But no, I flew in luxury, travelling in a 747 Jumbo jet, and landed under eight hours later, feeling fresh as a spring daisy and was met at arrivals by a highfalutin lawyer from Wall Street. As soon as I was out of the airport, I was given a full reading of my late aunt's will. A complete rundown, while we sat in the back of a stretch limo, drinking French brandy, smoking Cuban cigars on our way to the Mark Hotel, where I was booked into a luxurious suite. What I was informed next, I found it hard to accept, as this information was beyond my rational thinking. The lawyer told me I was now the CEO of a Fortune 500 company. And news, that ran a shock to my already excessively stressed system, an owner of more property that you could ever imagine and net wealth of 14 billion dollars. I owned real estate, banks, an airline, a steel production industry, shipping, energy and utilities, an oil company, electronic business and the business that started it all for my late aunt and uncle, YOHADOW, a multinational computer technology corporation headquartered in downtown Manhattan. And by some incredible luck, good fortune, fluke, or blessing, or whatever word could describe it, the group did not suffer the stock failure of Black Monday in 1987 as many substantial companies did. The group, YFG Corp, grew and grew. I was at the head of a conglomerate of continual success. My mind was full of business ideas, and I served the business empire as a father figure. And the company grew into the monster I now control at a distance.

"I no longer run the daily workings of the group, I leave all this work to my three sons from my second marriage, and luckily, I rediscovered my daughter from Scotland, and she also works and lives in New York, and is very much part of our family.

"I never lost connections with Glasgow, nor the people that showed me kindness. I had an honest opening to give my vast fortune to charitable causes, so I set up funds towards preventing, curing or managing all diseases. I made contributions to medical science, pledged money to combat oceanic degradation, as well as wildlife causes and gave significant contributions towards fighting HIV and AIDS (particularly in Africa). All this work was designed in a way. And that way was done in preparation, for this moment in time, a short brief window of the present day in Glasgow. The young woman we just left at her party, Violet Brook, is now in her late thirties, working in Africa on numerous essential causes. She works in war-torn countries, reducing malnutrition in children, improving access to a welfare system, working with other charities to supply malaria vaccines, she also works with many others to offer clean water and promote hygiene. The list is endless but worthy. Violet is now chairperson and head of the YOHADOW Foundation. She is not the type of person to sit in an office and make commands. Violet is boots on the ground. Heavily involved with every part of our philanthropy. Through her continuous hard work, she has saved the lives of millions and many millions more will benefit from her virtuous humanity.

Recently, I met with Jesus in New York, and with his love, he sent me to complete the Glasgow journey. A journey that will bring more changes to the souls of others, a new hope rises to keep strength within our hearts and a benevolent cause that will develop for all the people of Glasgow. We will tune into the essence of love which can provide a future with a brighter vision and give glory to the highest as we walk with the truth. This is your moment in time!"

Donald was lost for words. He struggled to find any suitable argument that could achieve a revelation which he hoped would unfurl his part in all this madness.

"I honestly do not understand what I can do. I have nothing to offer apart from myself."

Jonathon Dailly was quick to intervene.

"That's all you need, Donald. A bright and kind soul like yours can scatter precious smiles through the poorest of sad hearts. Just be, and always remain yourself."

Jonathan Dailly continued,

"I have already donated to heart of the homeless, and this will continue with more funds soon, we will enlarge the charity to cover funding for drop-in centres, new homes built on dedicated sites and extensive advice from qualified specialist advisors and increase a solid full-time base to help alleviate the suffering of the poorest people in the city.

"From my own point of view, I struggled many years ago with mental health, when I decided to take my life. The Clyde had accepted my weak body as its own, but thankfully, for the grace of God, you and the spirit of young Tommy Shaw, I was saved. For you now, any problem you find where social inequality is profound, where homeless need help, you must build productive relationships between the homeless and appropriate social services, and remain steadfast in every effort, or decision you make; to open a pathway, to develop a suicide Prevention Protocol that works for everyone. This will work with dedication and a strong will, which you have in abundance. Charitable money will be available for all of these incredible causes and more!

"However, on another point, something you have knowledge of. The young baby girl you recently viewed falling from the top floor of a tenement, on both occasions, had been coerced to sit on the window by two building workers. These workers were evil beings, placed in that situation to cause her injury or death; they chose death and thankfully failed with both efforts. They had two opportunities to do this, their first chance failed, and the 2nd time, one year to the day, followed the same path with the same result. The baby was safe! You laid witness to Ian Shaw saving the baby, yet, as weird and crazy this may sound, it was you that saved the baby."

Donald offered no response. He looked bewildered and mentally numb.

"We knew the challenge that faced us. But we were ready, our timeline link had to move into place, create a pattern where evil was unaware of our possible moves. This is where you, Donald, with close ties to the family, made miraculous moves to save the baby, again, on both occasions, you successfully saved the girl. That tiny baby would grow up to be Violet Brook. So you see, Donald, we must be cautiously aware that our family is protected as we go forth to provide people of love.

"You gave our timeline hope for the future. So you see, Donald, we are forever linked and together. Always remember, life is now as it will always be!"

Donald looked at the clock on the wall and time had remained as it was when both entered the cafe. The latte on the table was still hot as Jonathon Dailly raised the cup to his mouth, supped the milky coffee, and spoke,

"This is a really nice latte!"

Donald's taxi sat once again near George Square, on the confluence of George street. A keen look at his mobile phone, he realised it was 11.00 and it was Christmas Eve, and he was back in the present day, but to him, he had just awoken from a daydream. The snow had started, it fell heavy, he felt the day had finished and homeward bound was effectively the only impression imprinted on his mind.

A smart press of the starter button ignited the 2.5 ltr diesel engine which immediately ignited into action, and his right foot directly pumped the gas to rev the engine in preparation for a move forwards and a thankful return to the warmth of his home in Dennistoun. Just then, the passenger rear door opened, and an ageing man and a young, heavily pregnant woman entered the taxi.

"Can you take us to Ruthven Street please?" the man said in a jovial voice.

A few drinks have passed his lips, Donald thought. It's that Christmas spirit he kept hearing about.

"Of course."

The (on-hire) light was illuminated, and Donald made a few hasty manoeuvres in the direction needed, to get them to the west end of Glasgow. The couple chatted continually, and their good-humoured appearance showed much fun and laughter on their cold red faces.

The roads were quiet due to the heavy snow that was already resting a few inches deep which made safe driving difficult, as Donald drove slowly and carefully onward to counteract this added road hazard. Many minutes later, just as his cab neared the old Kelvin Bridge, a bird, a large black bird, in fact, a large black crow flew through the tunnel of on-coming snow towards the windscreen as Donald reacted immediately. Turning the steering wheel to the nearside road and actioning the emergency stop, a reaction which came naturally to him, to avoid hitting the bird. As his driving skills acted abruptly, Donald shouted the word very loud, "CROW!"

The taxi spun in semi-circles, one way, then the next, as it gained uncontrollable acceleration which threw the black cab and its passengers up and over the pavement to hit the green metal cast iron balustrade that sat firmly on the old bridge.

An incredibly forced stop that threw Donald and his two helpless passengers, with no escaping, ungainly around the interior of his taxi.

"What the hell is happening!" shouted the man in the cabin towards Donald.

"I have serious discomfort, Dad. The pain is horrific!" the girl screamed as she moaned and groaned louder, and continually promoted her distress, which scared her father and raised his anxiety levels to extreme heights.

"Driver, get in here and help. My daughter is pregnant and in pain!" the man bellowed instructions as if he was demanding Donald, with or without injury, to get a move on and help his daughter in any way he could.

The seatbelt that contained Donald was unclipped as he fled his cab making way into the rear cabin.

"When is the baby due?" was the only words his mind could fathom at this precise moment.

"Not till early January but that's not the issue, your driving has caused this. Can you please phone an ambulance?" the man spoke nervously.

"No!" the girl belted out several times and held back from profanities as the pain was nearing conclusion.

"You can't! I am having the baby now." She let out more shrieks and cries for help which planted her father and Donald into a surplus feeling of immediate distress.

"You sort it out. It was you that put my daughter into this state. This is an emergency so you will do everything possible," said the large Cro-Magnon man.

Donald's mind whirled in every direction as the man's voice reverberated through his sensitive ears, attempting to avoid any further words of instructions that came his way. However, he did hear the next few words, even over the screams of the anguished girl.

"YOU! It's bloody well YOU!"

The man's voice filled the cold night air and almost shook the taxi.

"You are the fool that stopped your taxi in front of my police van, and we nearly went through the windscreen. You are the bloody freak that thought you had run over Jesus and the Jesus guy was sitting in the back seat. Man, you are weird, and why on God's earth do I have the unfortunate luck to have you as our taxi driver," said the vocally active passenger.

"Shut up! Shut up!" the girl screamed as she lay stretched on the seat, breathing in as much oxygen her lungs could contain. "I'm having my baby!"

Both men looked at each other as the girl's screams and her heavy panting filled the taxi.

"It's coming, for God's sake!" she shrieked at a high pitch. "The baby is coming!" the girl yelled louder than before.

Donald was forcefully pushed forwards towards the girl as her father threw him near to where the girl sat. He succumbed to the occasion and made an exit to stand uncomfortably in the heavy snow. He felt more at ease away from the situation he could not cope with.

"I don't know what to do," said Donald tensely and irritatingly nervous. "I haven't done this before," he spoke tensely.

"Neither have I," she shrieked fully.

Within a moment, a baby's head appeared, then its small shoulders suddenly came into view, and Donald apprehensively cupped his hands around its little body as it fell gently into his arms with ease and with full comfort to the young mother.

"It's a girl!" he said with emotion in his voice as he repeated this several times to the girl that cried and laughed uncontrollably.

"My God, I cannot believe this. The baby is so beautiful," he said with strong emotion in his voice.

Donald gave the young mother her new-born baby and removed his warm coat to wrap around the small child. His next move was deliberate, but assured, as he opened the door to see the girl's father directing a paramedic into the taxi. Leaving the sanctuary of his cab to allow the specialists to do their job, Donald approached the off-duty police officer to offer his hand in congratulations on the birth of his granddaughter. The man was speechless yet overawed by the moment, he stuttered both vocally and physically but did eventually receive Donald's hand. Tightly seized, he shook it forcibly as he gripped Donald in a bear hug that had so much force, his breathing all but stopped.

"You are a saint for helping my daughter, and I thank you for everything. I must apologise for my unreasonable actions earlier, but if it wasn't for you, I really don't know how I could have coped."

The girl was already in the process of being transferred into the safety of the ambulance as its blue lights radiated like a beacon in the dark, snow-filled evening.

"I don't think I did anything special. It was so quick," Donald's voice shook as if lacking boldness of confidence.

"I just helped in any way I could, maybe a little bit," he added.

"You were fantastic, and I will make sure your taxi is fully repaired at my expense, that is something I can do to thank you," the large man said as he made his way into the rear of the ambulance as its doors were forcibly closed behind him as it began to move slowly back in the direction of the city centre. Lights still pulsated, and a siren sounded which added chaos and excitement to the situation.

Donald watched as the ambulance disappeared into the night, and his temperate curiosity gave added attention to the belief that a miracle had, once again, taken place. As he turned to observe his damaged taxi, he now saw it sitting correctly on the road and parallel with the pavement, and a quick walk around the vehicle showed no indication of damage. A miracle has been at play yet again, he fully assumed and accepted.

His cab was ticking over, and warm air filled the interior as he opened the back door to remove his great coat which he gladly put on. His goal was now high on his agenda, his aim now was to get home.

Who phoned the emergency service? How did they arrive so fast? The baby came on its own. Not with my help? I just held it and gave the mother her small child. These sentences ran through his mind as he drove homeward.

A full gaping yawn disturbed Donald's concentration as he drove through the on-going snowfall as he neared the city centre of Glasgow. But as he commanded the situation, and to take adequate control of the vehicle as it moved through heavy snow, he felt an unexpected spine-tingling moment. Looking at the mirror, his attention is drawn to the person sitting in the rear cabin, a person he recognised well, and it was Jesus, yet he wasn't the George Harrison lookalike he recently met, in fact, he looked like Jesus as most people observe his likeness. He looked like Jesus!

There was no fear, nor did Donald feel apprehensive in the circumstance he found himself, not now, not ever, there was a feeling of warmth and hope and love circulating through his veins as he waited for Jesus to speak.

"Take me to Mandela Place please, Donald," were the only words Jesus spoke on the short journey to the destination. Again and without any significant warning, both Jesus and Donald stood in the deep snow and faced the ornate, Timothy Schmaltz sculpture of a homeless Jesus that sits near St Georges Church in central Glasgow.

"Try your best, Donald. That is all I can ask of you. The homeless, the poor, the unforsaken, all need help. And with much effort, hope will rise. We can only raise others with the word of God, and if you just help one person at a time, then you have done well. Give hope to the many, Donald, and allow the less successful in gaining an appreciation of what many have, and easily accept for granted."

Jesus points his long, outstretched forefinger towards the statue.

"This creation observes the plight of people less fortunate, people that live under many different anxieties, and find themselves homeless and without care. Disadvantaged and free from society and social welfare that could help them, only to be left abandoned and vulnerable, and in a place where life has far too many obstacles lurking in the shadows that raises evil souls to masquerade as do-gooders. But you know different, Donald.

"Stop corruption in its process and help as many poor people you can.

"Truth never lies, it is only people that lie about the truth. Go forth and trust my words."

Donald felt a surge of warmth flow entirely through his body, as Jesus leant forwards and kissed him in the forehead. A smile of love from the son of God ended the brief meeting as Jesus started to walk from the scene and into the snow-filled night.

Behold

Donald sat peacefully in his taxi on George Square, it was Christmas Eve, and it was snowing. A few jolly revellers still enjoyed that last hour or so before midnight, catching a few last drinks, before a journey home before Christmas arrived, and that's where Donald and his fellow taxi drivers assisted the late-night partygoers.

He wondered how many people would attend church on this cold, yet festive eve?

A moment of surprise allowed him to be awakened from his daydream as the back door of the cab clicked open.

"Am I glad to see you! I have phoned you for hours and got no response. Have you been OK?" said the highly-dressed woman as she made herself comfortable on the leather-bound seat.

"Yes," he said turning to face the woman. "My phone must have a battery fault as I didn't hear it ring," he paused as he gained to focus on the passenger.

"Shona, it's you!" cheerfully said Donald in a bewildered state.

"Yes, who do you think I was going to be? Jesus?" she said mockingly.

Donald's mind was clear of the recent apostolic miracles his life endured, his brain absorbed many new memories he may or may not have lived, but many fresh recollections flooded the frontal lobe of his cerebral cortex which gave him insight to where his life currently stood and presented him an idea to his life experiences at present.

"I'm sorry, Shona, I forgot you had a party meal with the staff tonight. How did it go?" he asked in an informed way.

"It went well. Everyone is asking for you and very excited about you helping at the start of the new year. It's all looking very good, Donald, What a turnaround for the charity. Oh! I spoke with Alison, she and her husband are at the flat waiting for us to return. I believe they ordered fast food, so no need to cook when we get home," she kept speaking as her voice began to filter into a faint chat, talking about many conversations she had at the party, but Donald didn't respond as her voice became distant.

The taxi was on its way home as Donald had further clear memories of his close relationship with Shona, in fact, very close, and had been for over a year, considering they married during the summer past and spent a month-long honeymoon on the Caribbean island of Barbados. Happy recollections came flooding back, he saw images of a beautiful beach where both watched laughing gulls hover in the cloudless blue sky as they flew above the clear turquoise ocean. Memories now clear as day. He knew his daughter, Alison, and her French boyfriend, Pierre, were coming to stay over the Christmas holidays, which added enjoyment to the end of year surprise he prayed for. He felt as if his brain had been rebooted back to reality he wasn't sure ever existed. But here he was, and it all felt real enough.

The drive home was short, and now Donald and Shona began chatting like tweeting songbirds about many subjects, mainly Christmas dinner, drinks, TV shows, meeting family and friends, homeless charity work and having a rare old time over the celebrations!

Donald forgot all his recent religious experiences except one. As his taxi parked under a nearby lamppost opposite his apartment, for some strange reason, he remembered a card in his coat pocket. A card received from a mysterious woman, or a fortune telling machine possibly – though could not remember when, where, or why this reading had taken place. All he could recall was a simple question he asked, and this card would reveal the secret, give a truthful answer to his question.

Without hacking his brain, he remembered an old music hall machine which answered questions, and distant memory suggested her name was Madame Zita, so he asked,

"Who answers all of the questions?"

His fingers fumbled through his pockets that finally produced a worn card, a very faded and delicate ticket, many years had withered the paper, yet it was still in remarkable condition and readable. He focussed on the card.

It said; 'Jesus does.'

A confused and perplexed look appeared over his face, why he would ask a machine this question, and why is it relevant at all?

"Are you coming, Donald? It's a wild night out here!" Shona questioned him and broke his moment of substantial thoughts as he sat reclining in the driver seat staring at the small note.

"Yes, I'm coming!" he said, as he soon followed Shona over the snow-covered road to the safety of his home, as a high pitch beep and coloured lights flashed behind him confirming the taxi had locked.

Christmas in
Donald's Apartment

Donald stared from his window into the icy white dark night. Watching intently at the strange man that had stood quiet in the snow for an extended period, enter a long black limousine, then it drove off gently into the enduring blizzard. Boisterous applause behind him gave sudden knowledge that Christmas day had arrived, and with normality beckoned within him, he immediately returned to the family party where his daughter forced a glass of cold fizzy champagne into his hand.

"Merry Christmas, Dad!"

"Merry Christmas, everybody!" Donald smiled and shouted as he moved close to hug and kiss his wife and daughter.

As the morning progressed, it moved happily on, in a joyful and celebratory way. A pleasant and long-awaited reunion with his daughter was well overdue, and a full catch up was expanding as information flew from his long-estranged daughter. *This is the tonic I needed*, he said to himself. He spent extended time chatting with his new son-in-law, Pierre Comtois, who enthralled Donald when hearing a brief history of his family. Formerly from Picardy in Northern France, the eldest child of Henry and Marianne Comtois, both his parents operate and run their own small, yet fashionable, champagne house, a brand called the Templar and the Cross. He further explained that the golden fizz dancing in his glass was, in fact, the family's best vintage from 1996, a dazzling, ripe and intense structured and likely long-lived classic champagne which made him smile in appreciation of the delicious, palatable wine. And that a case was already stored in the kitchen for further celebrations which made his smile more full.

The young man continued his story. He moved to Paris to work for Police Nationale as a Captain in the Service de protection des Hautes personalities [SPHP] where his command operated VIP security such as foreign diplomats and protection for the President of the French Republic.

It was with his job he met and fell in love with Alison, who managed a small boutique hotel near the city centre. All of this happened ten years previously, and they married shortly afterwards in the Scottish Kirk in Paris that sits smugly on Rue Bayard.

Donald felt he had missed so much, especially his own daughter's wedding, a child he hadn't seen since she was six years of age. Though comfortable in listening more, Alison produced a leather satchel of wedding photos and images of their up-market apartment owned by Pierre's parents. The deluxe, penthouse property was in the Marais district of Paris, a place of prestige where many trendy Parisians spent many social hours mingling at the art conclave of stylish bars and cafes, and both Shona and Donald participated willingly in hearing more of the continuing life story of the young couple.

As the information built to a crescendo, and all glasses had been charged with overflowing 'Templar and the Cross' bubbly, Alison handed a small box to her father and spoke,

"Before you open the box, Dad, I have a short speech to make."

She paused for a moment.

"Since we haven't been in each other's lives for many years, and the truth is that I could not trace you anywhere in Glasgow, including the multitude of times I tried to find you through many available avenues. Or speak with online social media groups attempting to solve the mystery of what had happened to my father. Pierre tried numerous times using resources I could only dream of having access to, but not one lead came to fruition."

She paused again and stared at her husband looking for assurance. He nodded in agreement to allow her to continue.

"We found you, though purely by chance. We finished work early one week and made a 100 km drive north to spend a long weekend at Pierre's parent's winery. On Saturday evening, their annual party was in full flow with family, guests and distinguished clientele, including their local Mayor, drunk and happily telling dirty jokes to anyone that would listen, among fifty or so guests. It was a big occasion, an end of season grape harvest was always a gathering not to be missed. And this one became so much distinctive and unique to any other. We still don't actually believe the full extent of the story."

Alison made a move for a seat and the look on her dad's face, which had a similar expectant look to his wife, Shona's, waited in bated breath as Alison made herself comfortable.

"We did the family thing. Mingled with guests, chatted about everything under the sun, and many conversations got loud and annoying I can tell you, though we just smiled and listened, as free champagne kept flowing. That is until Sacha arrived, he is Pierre's father. With him, he brought a client, in fact, an extremely wealthy American businessman who in short, is one, if not the largest, purchasers of the family's champagne, was introduced to us. He spoke fluent French, and we were suddenly awestruck by the man, his stories, his humour, his intellect was mind-blowing, his manners were impeccable and this man of copious wealth had not one pretentious bone in his body. An outright gentleman if we ever had the grace to meet. This man never bored us at any point. Even his mention of the global business empire he owned, it never felt ludicrous or pompous listening to him explain details of this.

"Then, in a flash, he began to tell a story of how his fortune was made.

"A story that was way beyond fiction and a surplus tale that lay somewhere between creation and freakish masterly invention which would more than likely be the location to embed this weird and unearthly account of his life.

"He explained, he had been happily married with a family, had a well-earned good job, lived as a loving father and husband, and one day, changed. His life collapsed around him.

"Mixing with the wrong people, taking drugs and alcohol, losing the most essential part of his life, his family, then suddenly, all gone. In a flash, he was homeless and living on the streets of Glasgow.

"I intervened his account loudly in English, 'Glasgow?'

"To which he replied in English, 'Yes, Glasgow, my home town.' I explained that I was born there and left with my mother to live in Cornwall at the age of six.

"We diverted briefly about Scotland, and his love for the country and its people.

"We were surprised but fascinated that this decent man ventured to tell two strangers, a full committed narrative over the darkest period of his life. And possibly an experience that many Wall Street journals or the venerable New York Times would love to have access to, a personal revelation of one of America's wealthiest people, was now being allocated to myself and Pierre.

"He detailed his life when he was at his lowest, deeply consumed with hatred and hurt, void of hope and ambition, by events that terrorised his state of mind, which he did not repeat or give reason why, yet his last choice, a choice to end his life would be a decision of his own making. A choice he made, an opportunity he felt appropriate for the circumstance he found himself. And that choice, however far it lay from his past beliefs or former reality, a life he now had, had to be deleted. An experience he would gladly give up!

"He continued his incredible story with him standing alone, on a parapet of a bridge in Glasgow, preparing to jump. Then, he revealed an unbelievable family link. It was you, Dad. He spoke of a kind-hearted man he remembered who he talked openly as his life slithered away, the man listened honestly to his distressed feelings and gave a small grasp of hope to his dwindling life. The man bent on saving him called himself Donald Forbes.

"We were shocked; could this man be the same Donald Forbes we had relentlessly search for.

"But it gets as eerie as anyone would ever believe. Trust me, this is mind-blowing!

"Finally, the businessman added, the man that jumped into the river to save him had left his coat on the bridge before attempting a rescue. When he was finally liberated, someone threw a coat into the ambulance, believing it was his. And he further stated, which I find unfathomable to even comprehend, that when he arrived in America for the first time, the suite in the hotel he was registered had the same coat, dry-cleaned and hanging in the wardrobe with a small box full of items found in its pockets.

"Now, Dad, I offer you a chance to take a large mouthful of champagne to repress your senses, with what surprising announcement I am about to tell you."

In tandem, Donald and Shona excitedly emptied remnants of their glasses with whole mouthfuls as Pierre served prompt refills, in anticipation to hear the conclusion to this story. They were intrigued to hear more.

Alison, guided by many rehearsals of the story, sat back, filled her glass and took a sip which cleansed her palate and eased her dry mouth.

"A few weeks later, we received a parcel delivery. A large box with an attached letter. Of course, the message was from the American businessman. In this letter were full and intricate details of the bridge incident and the coat, your coat, Dad. He explained, he did a similar search for you and only discovered recently, you were working with a local Glasgow Charity, Have a heart for the Homeless.

"Dad, I need to ask you a question. Did you ever save the life of Jonathon Dailly, or ever meet this man?"

The look on Donald's face gave an impression he wasn't sure of the name, but before he could respond Shona intervened.

"I'm sure the American businessman now funding our charity is a man called Jonathon Dailly. I'm sure that's his name. In fact, yes! It is Jonathon Dailly, but this could be someone else with the same name," offered Shona.

"I never saved anyone in my life. I am not a great swimmer, so I guess he must have got my old coat from somewhere else, and information with my identity was in it. But I never jumped into the Clyde to save him or anyone else, that's for sure," positively delivered Donald.

"Do you have a black coat?" Alison question her father.

"Yes, it is in the hallway," Donald said as he rose and walked to the hall to collect his coat.

The participants waited a few moments until Donald arrived, clutching his long, knee-length coat. After checking his inside zipped pocket, an item was produced.

"My wallet!" Donald rummaged all the coat's pockets and laid each item on the coffee table that centred the room.

"Chewing gum, mints and some old wrappers. But definitely my coat."

The coat was opened from the inside to reveal his name written boldly on a lapel patch.

"My coat. A coat I have had for years!" said positively and proudly assured.

Alison was already in the process of opening the box she had arrived with. A groan of shock left the mouths of the small group engaging in this materialistic conundrum.

A long, black coat was held aloft, Donald's eyes were scanning every inch of the overcoat, looking as if he has seen a ghost as Alison opened the jacket to show Donald's name imprinted on the label as his own coat. An exact replica in every detail. A full reaction of bewilderment soon followed, and Donald took the overcoat and matched both together but could not see any difference. Even a few small holes he knew existed, sat in the same places, the cuffed sleeves were accurate, wear and tear matched as humanly possible, and for whatever reason, he could not honestly say which coat was his.

"When we received this box over a month ago, there was something in else in the pocket," said Alison as she produced an opened envelope where she revealed and presented a card, a Christmas card.

"This card was sent to you, Dad, around mid-December, and when we spoke from the airport yesterday, you said you had just received it in the morning post, and crazy to say, yesterday was Christmas Eve."

She handed the card to her father and continued,

"So how on earth could the stranger send me a Christmas card, a card that I hadn't sent, even before I purchased it. It is the card, isn't it?" She held it out for Donald to view at close range. He nodded and spoke, "It looks exactly like the card you sent me." He paused to collect his thoughts. "I have that card, it's in my cab. I have it sellotaped to the dashboard. It was a Christmas greeting from my beautiful daughter, and I wanted it close by. This is an incredible duplicate and what does all of this mean?"

The group relaxed and inhaled air to give thoughts on this occurrence, though not one of them felt fear or were anxious with this extraordinary mystery.

"This additional card, also found in a pocket, do you know what this is?" Alison said as she handed the small paper ticket to her father.

"Madame Zita Fortune Teller," he said and forever forgot the rationale of the previous memory, as he read one side of the note. Turning it around, the card stated: 'Life is now as it will always be!'

"Well, that isn't mine," he said loudly. "I have never had my fortune read, ever! I don't have a clue where that came from."

"The note Jonathon Dailly sent, finished with a few lines that I want to read now, Dad. Maybe this will put closure to this fanciful mystery.

"Dear Donald, the time has passed ever so slightly, yet ever so far, since we briefly met that day on the bridge.

"I thank you for saving my life, and help me find a purpose for my existence and well-being. You are a true man of light and when you talked kindly to me all these years ago, words that are forever imprinted in my memory. You said these words; Think about your family and friends. Then you added these simple words to form an unforgettable sentence – Maybe the best is yet to come!

"Those words came to me in the water. I swallowed mouthfuls of frozen disgusting water, I was dying, I was on a short trip to death. But when you came to my rescue, with a young police officer called Ian Shaw, and the ghost of Young Tommy, together, you gave me trust in life once more. All four of us connected with our own unique experience. I heard your words as you floated away from my rescue. You shouted; Maybe the best is yet to come!

"I heard this sentence again and again as it forced adrenalin to pump through my veins and give me another chance at life, and by living, I had to convey this message to many, not the few, but help others, less fortunate than my sorrowful soul. Thankfully, with your help, I survived. And now currently, God's time, it is coming into place. For this, I thank you."

Alison stopped and prepared to offer more of Jonathon Dailly's words. Something more unimaginable, something explainable as paranormal or something that transcended the supernatural realism that may, or may not, co-exist with human normality was about to be spoken.

"He ended his letter with this strange postscript.

"A timeline of sorts, a list of 13 people from the present day to late 11th Century. He signed the letter, forever your friends. The list from the present day back in time is as follows; Jonathon Dailly (as we know, a Billionaire financier of many charitable causes), Charles Law, AE Pickard (owner of Glasgow Panopticon Theatre), Rev Edward Bayne, Judge Oliver Leary, Captain Duncan Stewart, Raymond Hogan, Thomas McIvor, Oliver Smollet, James Morton, William Shaw and Richard Comtois.

"After serious web searches, I soon discovered a few of these matching names were people based in Scotland, apart from Richard Comtois from the 11th century. Let me explain.

"Richard Comtois. Richard was born at Chateau de ficelle d'or, or translated in English, the Castle of Golden String. This ancient ruin still sits on the land of Richards parent's vineyard, and with inquisitive ancestry research, we discovered that Richard Comtois was born in 1075. His father, Richard Snr, was a significant landowner in Picardy and a proud servant of Lord Baldwin Des Marets, and agreed wholeheartedly for his son to serve his army on the road to Jerusalem to fight in the 1st Crusade in 1099. The young man was never traced and probably killed in battle. And this Comtois family are the direct descendants of Pierre!

"Additional research showed three more likely results. Firstly, we checked for a Captain Duncan Stewart, and only a brief perusal of the UK national archives, a Capt. D Stewart was registered as a sea Captain and businessman who founded the Stewart shipping line in 1780. He resided in Leith, near Edinburgh. He and his wife, Emily, worked tirelessly to serve people in Edinburgh's Poor House which was mostly financed by church-door and voluntary donations. On the death of a young mother, an inmate in the poor house, during childbirth, Duncan and his wife legally adopted the baby boy and raised him as their own. He gave all his fortunes to serve the poor.

"And the next person on the list that came up positive during a search was Rev Edward Bayne, a Church of Scotland minister based in Glasgow.

"In the 1830s, he had witnessed significant cholera outbreaks in Glasgow and other areas of Scotland, affecting all ages and classes of society. From the effects of poor living conditions among the lower levels of the social order, they suffered the most. He spent most of his non-ministerial time working aimlessly to help the cities poor. He died of cholera related disease at the age of 29. History records this man as benevolent and kind, and a man the poor remembered.

"To find A E Pickard was an easy search online. The eccentric showman owned Glasgow's Britannia Panopticon music hall theatre, strangely enough, the man that gave young Stan Laurel his first break into comedy and his first ever stage appearance. This man also had a heart of gold. He owned many properties which were rented accommodation for unfortunate families. He never once threw a tenant out of any of his property and always gave generously to people who needed help. He gave secretively copious amounts of money to charity.

"What I see from the research is that from the truth discovered, related to each person who dedicated their time, wealth and efforts, generously to help others, so much less fortunate than themselves. If any of this is accurate, and far be it for me to make any professional or knowledgeable conclusion on it, I would hasten to add that this is a mystery that will never be solved with reason. That is why I believe this story will be a story without an ending."

Christmas morning adjourned, and all packed up their thoughts and unanswered questions and took them all to bed. Then individual dreams took over to make each person view a journey of revelation. Dreams that signified the ultimate proof that life is now as will always be. When morning arrived and breakfast served, sleepy heads gathered with no memory of the strange occurrences of early morning. The black coat had disappeared along with the irritating, mind-blowing circumstances that had swamped their brains with the knowledge they could never contemplate maintaining. This whole story of events vanished as quick as it appeared. Yet… Alison spoke,

"Let's open our presents now!" She moved fast towards the tree and brought bundles to the table as all looked for the present with their name attached. "One for you, Shona, it's from Dad." And Pierre had already opened his present which was a silver Quaich and a bottle of the finest malt whisky.

"Wow, so much appreciated, guys. Thank you so much." He added a French sentence, "*C'est tellement apprecie.*"

"My God, Donald. How on earth did you know I always wanted this?" said Shona full of childish excitement and joy. "A Valentino embroidered hooded jacket. I just love this." She jumped to her feet and put the jacket over her pyjamas to loud applause, and she hugged and gave Donald a long slobbery kiss on his forehead. "That is too much money, Donald, you should never have done this, but I'm not arguing the fact. It's gorgeous! Thank you, thank you, thank you!" she screamed and shouted.

"Dad, you should never have done this either. It must be so expensive!" Alison said producing a typed voucher for a holiday for two to St Lucia. First class flights from Paris, Luxury five-star beach hotel and £1000 expenses. "This is amazing, thank you so much!"

"I missed your wedding and even though you have had a honeymoon, I put money aside for years, and now it is time to spend it, it's the least I can do."

Donald opened his Christmas gifts and reacted in a similar way to the others. He loved his new wallet, his Maurice Lacroix watch, a supercar race day at Knockhill and an invite to Pierre's parent's next harvest party for both Donald and Shona.

All done and dusted, the day grew onward, and food and drink vanished as quick as it was served, TV took over the agenda, as did coffee and tea, chocolates and pudding, and all was well in Dennistoun. Donald stood and raised his glass and shouted,

"A Merry Christmas and a happy new year to all! For the future and the past!"

The End Nearly

"Donald, there is still a present here, and your name is on it," said Shona, passing it to him as he sat cosy in his seat, in relaxed comfort near to the wall mounted flat television screen that presented a program of church carol singers.

The wrapping paper was ripped off at pace, disregarded in a bundle at his feet and the lid removed to show a small black Hackney cab. He took the toy from the box, wearing a silly grin on his face, he said a few grateful thanks to whoever gave him this fantastic present, though no one admitted to being the benefactor. He held it up for all to see. A toy Hackney cab with a driver, a passenger in the rear and a number plate that read: J3 SUS.

"Your taxi has Jesus in the back!" they laughed, but still, no one would admit to giving this present. But he loved it just as much as his other gifts.

"Well, let's drink to my new and beautiful present. And whichever of you guys bought this toy, I can only thank you in one way.

"I've got Jesus in the back of my taxi!"

All was well in his apartment. A Heart for The Homeless charity grew and grew, and many more associate homeless and suicidal charitable groups set in motion a movement that would see Glasgow become a leading light for social conscience. A new time was emerging in Glasgow.

The End

Epilogue

Obviously, within this tale, there are questions yet to be answered. You will be wondering if specific issues were put right, or actions taken to set everything that happened through Donald's journey were made acceptable and believable, then a full conclusion could be made of this historic declaration. Or possibly an ambition to learn facts about the narrator, and why I have a distinct knowledge of Donald's timeline. If you read on, I will put closure on these simple, yet gloriously outlandish facts. However, once you have read these proofs, you will eventually lose all memories of them.

I trust you are still inquisitively curious.

Okay, let me explain a few histories and how they panned out.

Here are a few endings which give closure on past participants that played more than a part in Donald's meaningful life.

Ian Shaw, the affable retired police officer, eventually moved to St Andrews, with his daughter, her partner and his much-loved granddaughter, Angel Holly Short. They joyfully settled and soon became established residents within the town. Working for local charities and many, many worthwhile benevolent causes, they raised thousands of pounds over many years, and, of course, he always managed to have a regular game of golf, and in all honesty, that's the main reason of moving there. Life in the future would see his granddaughter become one of the first female chief constables in Scotland. Within the force, she would work closely with rape victims and establish specialist units devoted to the investigation of rape. Her policing methods would be copied by many authorities with great success throughout the free world.

Both forever dancing, Edna and her friend, Colin McDonald, travelled on many affordable cruise holidays, as anyone could fit into a calendar year, to enjoy their remaining life together. Their dancing prowess became so critically acclaimed and highly admired by crew and passengers alike, they were offered a job tutoring dance over a full season for a Baltic Cruise company, which they accepted. Many more working years followed our delightfully, rhythmic performers, as they danced in the beam of the main spotlight gloriously on many major cruise liners.

Miss Turner, Donald's young, energetic teacher of a time past, took her superior communication skills to Africa in early 1973. Her work became dedicated to rescue injured and distressed animals, which, after valuable veterinary diagnosis and specialist treatment, the animals spent a lengthy rehabilitation, before being released back to the wild. Her ambassadorial skills and work with endangered species are well-documented, televised interviews became a regular occurrence, and at one point, a Hollywood movie was made about her working life. A film which launched the career of a young American movie star, Hilary Walton and made Lorna Turner gain international fame as a renowned animal activist. Her biography (I was made for saving animals) – the title of the movie, which in turn, promoted her generous charity effort to a larger audience.

AHA, Ark Haven Africa, based in several African countries, works tirelessly to help all animals. Elephants, rhinos, lions, giraffe and other remarkable wild animals in Africa are struggling, mainly due to diminishing reserve resources, the poaching calamity and a lack of wild space are all having catastrophic effects. Lorna Turner stood tall among her critics and forced many government bodies to act firmly on behalf of the animals, and many did.

Many years later, she met and befriended a younger fellow Scot, the spirited and angelic enterprising woman, Violet Brook. They are still good friends.

Finally, a mystery everyone needs full closure on, and that is the clandestine shadow angel, the bearer of gifts, at young Tommy Shaw's grave. Never seen, nor positive identity is proven, this elusive night-stalker would permanently pay homage to the hidden history of a crippled dead boy from Dennistoun. And the devoted and dedicated fellow visitor, a solitary crow, which was enduringly visible to any inquisitive taphophile, Tommy Shaw's feathered friend soon became an internet sensation, as did the story of the strange, mysterious visitor. So, who are they?

Understanding this may need another full analysis of the story, so if you are unsure of this explanation, read again.

Anyway, the shadow Angel is no other than A E Pickard! Strange, I agree, but as you well know, if you read to believe, then, 'Life is now as it will always be!' will remain a solid truth, a truth that cannot be broken, by man or evil.

It is always now!

So, who is solitary crow? Well, that is easy. It is me! As is the Balmanno Express conductor and the Nostalgia barman.

I am everywhere I need to be, and where I always ought to be, but places where I shouldn't be, I never walk that road.

Maybe we will meet soon on the path of the righteous.

I take it you want to know who sent Donald the toy taxi? I can tell you he was someone that helped shape Donald's timeline, a family connection that is not visibly obvious, but someone at the outset was as sceptical and cynical as anyone could be, but well-entangled in this story. And this man was, none other than, Ian Shaw. During Donald's journey with Jesus, Ian went on a similar trip, both unaware of each other's travels. So, just remember this, choose your trip well, make sure you decide the road you travel is truthful and recognised with sincere conviction, after all, every journey ends at the same destination. Besides, which may sound extraordinary weird and confusing, but both Donald and Ian Shaw saved young Violet's life. In cooperation together, simultaneously, yet, on other realms or plains and distinctly identical in every way, they succeeded in progressing the timeline. Ian Shaw was on the same journey as Donald, at the exact same time.

In fact, I could have named Ian as the main character in this story and had Donald play an observer. Whatever way it happened, the outcome would always remain the same. Life is now as it will always be.

Before I go, there is an important fact missing, and one I am sure you would be delighted to know. It was the time Donald sat in the taxi and a young woman smashed a handful of greasy chips onto the window which made him jump, was only correct to a point. You see, Donald had lain dead in his seat for a few minutes after a massive heart attack took his life. It was only then, the moment Jesus stepped into the taxi, that Donald felt he had awoken from a daydream, the dream of heaven was suspended for another day. And his journey was about to begin.

Before I go, here is the latest addition to Tommy's nautical rhymes, a Robert Ferguson poem:

It's peaceful now
This place to hide
Held forever
In its tide
Small voices echo
Where dreams reside
In darkened depths
Of the River Clyde.

Time

Days passed, seasons passed and years run forever forwards. Yet, time itself may be an illusion, it may be something special to give others, but only time can reconcile what reason cannot. The trouble is, we all believe we have time.
Faithfully yours,
Eae

Stranger Than Fact

When near completion of this novel, during some additional research online, looking for charitable causes in Glasgow to view as comparison, my eyes caught a glimpse of the Think Again campaign.

This safety and suicide prevention campaign was led by a Glasgow taxi driver and poet by the name Stef Shaw (purely coincidental) who writes under the title, the Glasgow Cabbie.

The successful movement for emergency phone lines on the Clyde evolved and extended to a River Clyde Memorial Event which pays tribute to all who have lost their lives to the River Clyde on Glasgow Green on the 30th June 2019.

Further details rapidly emerged, within Stef's s charitable work and connection to the welfare of the homeless, deaths occurring in the Clyde, his honest approach to continually working to have emergency phone lines installed on the banks of the River Clyde makes him a genuine and sedulous man of hope. A real mystery abides.

Maybe particle intervention is not so strange at all!

The End